MIDWIVES ON-CALL

Welcome to Melbourne Victoria Hospital—
and to the exceptional midwives
who make up the Melbourne Maternity Unit!

These midwives in a million work miracles
on a daily basis, delivering tiny bundles of joy
into the arms of their brand-new mums!

Amidst the drama and emotion of babies
arriving at all hours of the day and night, when
the shifts are over, somehow there's still time
for some sizzling out-of-hours romance…

Whilst these caring professionals might come
face-to-face with a whole lot of love in their
line of work, now it's their turn to find
a happy-ever-after of their own!

Midwives On-Call

*Midwives, mothers and babies—
lives changing for ever…!*

Dear Reader,

For me, there's no more powerful emotion than witnessing the miracle of birth. As a kid on a farm, birth never ceased to leave me amazed and awed, and that feeling's stayed with me all my life. So when I was asked to contribute to the *Midwives On-Call* anthology I jumped at the chance.

But my heroine has fertility issues, and as I wrote these questions drifted through my writing—what makes a parent? What makes love? Five years ago grief drove my hero and heroine apart. How much love does it take to bring them back together?

The midwives of Melbourne Victoria Hospital are a tight-knit team, facing the complexities of birth and love—and sometimes grief and loss—as part of their working day world. Life and death, love and joy—they're what matters. In the Melbourne Maternity Unit we see those emotions every time our midwives walk through the door, so it's only fitting that my lovers can finally find the power to love again.

Families take many forms. I hope you love the crazy, mixed-up bunch of loving that my Oliver and my Emily end up with.

Enjoy!

Marion

MEANT-TO-BE FAMILY

BY
MARION LENNOX

First published in Great Britain 2015
by Mills & Boon, an imprint of Harlequin (UK) Limited,
Large Print edition 2015
Eton House, 18-24 Paradise Road,
Richmond, Surrey, TW9 1SR

© 2015 Harlequin Books S.A.

Special thanks and acknowledgement are given
to Marion Lennox for her contribution to the
Midwives On-Call series

ISBN: 978-0-263-25505-8

Harlequin (UK) Limited's policy is to use papers that are natural, renewable and recyclable products and made from wood grown in sustainable forests. The logging and manufacturing processes conform to the legal environmental regulations of the country of origin.

Printed and bound in Great Britain
by CPI Antony Rowe, Chippenham, Wiltshire

Books by Marion Lennox

Mills & Boon® Medical Romance™

A Secret Shared...
Waves of Temptation
Gold Coast Angels: A Doctor's Redemption
Miracle on Kaimotu Island
The Surgeon's Doorstep Baby

Mills & Boon® Cherish™

Christmas Where They Belong
Nine Months to Change His Life
Christmas at the Castle
Sparks Fly with the Billionaire
A Bride for the Maverick Millionaire

**Visit the author profile page at
millsandboon.co.uk for more titles**

With thanks to my fellow authors,
who've helped make this *Midwives On-Call*
series fabulous. A special thank-you to
Alison Roberts, for her friendship, her
knowledge and her generosity
in sharing, and to Fiona McArthur,
whose midwife skills leave me awed.

MIDWIVES ON-CALL

Midwives, mothers and babies—
lives changing for ever...!

**Enter the magical world of the Melbourne Maternity Unit and
the exceptional midwives there, delivering tiny bundles of joy on a
daily basis. Now it's time to find a happy-ever-after of their own...**

Just One Night? by Carol Marinelli
Gorgeous Greek doctor Alessi Manos is determined
to charm the beautiful yet frosty Isla Delamere...
but can he melt this ice queen's heart?

Meant-To-Be Family by Marion Lennox
When Dr Oliver Evans's estranged wife, Emily, crashes back
into his life, old passions are re-ignited. But brilliant Dr Evans
is in for a surprise... Emily has two foster-children!

Always the Midwife by Alison Roberts
Midwife Sophia Toulson and hard-working paramedic
Aiden Harrison share an explosive attraction...but will they overcome
their tragic pasts and take a chance on love?

Midwife's Baby Bump by Susanne Hampton
Hot-shot surgeon Tristan Hamilton's passionate night
with pretty student midwife Flick has unexpected consequences!

Midwife...to Mum! by Sue MacKay
Free-spirited locum midwife Ally Parker
meets top GP and gorgeous single dad Flynn Reynolds.
Is she finally ready to settle down with a family of her own?

His Best Friend's Baby by Susan Carlisle
When beautiful redhead Phoebe Taylor turns up on ex-army medic
Ryan Matthews's doorstep there's only one thing keeping them apart:
she's his best friend's widow...and eight months pregnant!

Unlocking Her Surgeon's Heart by Fiona Lowe
Brooding city surgeon Noah Jackson
meets compassionate Outback midwife Lilia Cartwright.
Could Lilia be the key to Noah's locked-away heart?

Her Playboy's Secret by Tina Beckett
Renowned English obstetrician Darcie Green
might think playboy Lucas Elliot is nothing but trouble—
but is there more to this gorgeous doc than meets the eye?

Experience heartwarming emotion and pulse-racing drama in
Midwives On-Call
**this sensational eight-book continuity
from Mills & Boon Medical Romance**

**These books are also available in eBook format
from millsandboon.co.uk**

CHAPTER ONE

LATE. LATE, LATE, LATE. This was the third morning this week. Her boss would have kittens.

Not that Isla was in the mood to be angry, Em thought, as she swiped her pass at the car-park entry. The head midwife for Melbourne's Victoria Hospital had hardly stopped smiling since becoming engaged. She and her fiancé had been wafting around the hospital in a rosy glow that made Em wince.

Marriage. 'Who needs it?' she demanded out loud, as she swung her family wagon through the boom gates and headed for her parking spot on the fifth floor. She should apply for a lower spot—she always seemed to be running late—but her family wagon needed more space than the normal bays. One of the Victoria's obstetricians rode a bike. He was happy to park his Harley to one side of his bay, so this was the perfect arrangement.

Except it was on the fifth floor—and she was late again.

The car in front of her was slow going up the ramp. *Come on...* She should have been on the wards fifteen minutes ago. But Gretta had been sick. Again.

Things were moving too fast. She needed to take the little girl back to the cardiologist, but the last time she'd taken her, he'd said...

No. Don't go there. *There* was unthinkable. She raked her fingers through her unruly curls, trying for distraction. She'd need to pin her hair up before she got to the ward. Had she remembered pins?

It didn't work. Her mind refused to be distracted, and the cardiologist's warning was still ringing in her ears.

'Emily, I'm sorry, but we're running out of time.'

Was Gretta's heart condition worsening, or was this just a tummy bug? The little girl had hugged her tight as she'd left, and it had been all she could do to leave her. If her mum hadn't been there... But Adrianna adored being a gran. 'Get into work, girl, and leave Gretta to me. Toby and I will watch

Play School while Gretta has a nap. I'll ring you if she's not better by lunchtime. Meanwhile, go!'

She'd practically shoved her out the door.

But there *was* something wrong—and she knew what it was. The cardiologist had been blunt and she remembered his assessment word for word.

It was all very well, hearing it, she thought bleakly, but seeing it… At the weekend she'd taken both kids to their favourite place in the world, the children's playground at the Botanic Gardens. There was a water rill there that Gretta adored. She'd crawled over it as soon as she could crawl, and then she'd toddled and walked.

Six months ago she'd stood upright on the rill and laughed with delight as the water had splashed over her toes. At the weekend she hadn't even been able to crawl. Em had sat on the rill with her, trying to make her smile, but the little girl had sobbed. She knew what she was losing.

Don't! Don't think about it! Move on. Or she'd move on if she could.

'Come on.' She was inwardly yelling at the car in front. The car turned the corner ponderously then—praise be!—turned into a park on Level Four. Em sighed with relief, zoomed up the last ramp and hauled the steering wheel left, as she'd done hundreds of times in the past to turn into her parking space.

And...um...stopped.

There was a car where Harry's bike should be. A vintage sports car, burgundy, gleaming with care and polish.

Wider than a bike.

Instead of a seamless, silent transition to park, there was the appalling sound of metal on metal.

Her wagon had a bull bar on the front, designed to deflect stray bulls—or other cars during minor bingles. It meant her wagon was as tough as old boots. It'd withstand anything short of a road train.

The thing she'd hit wasn't quite as tough.

She'd ripped the side off the sports car.

Oliver Evans, gynaecologist, obstetrician and in-utero surgeon, was gathering his briefcase and his suit jacket from the passenger seat. He'd be meeting the hospital bigwigs today so he needed to be formal. He was also taking a moment to glance through the notes he had on who he had to meet, who he needed to see.

He vaguely heard the sound of a car behind him. He heard it turning from the ramp…

The next moment the passenger side of his car was practically ripped from the rest.

It was a measure of Em's fiercely practised calm that she didn't scream. She didn't burst into tears. She didn't even swear.

She simply stared straight ahead. Count to ten, she told herself. When that didn't work, she tried twenty.

She figured it out, quite quickly. Her parking spot was supposed to be wider but that was because she shared the two parking bays with Harry the obstetrician's bike and Harry had left. Of course. She'd even dropped in on his farewell party last Friday night, even though it had only been for five minutes because the kids had been waiting.

So Harry had left. This car, then, would belong to the doctor who'd taken his place.

She'd just welcomed him by trashing his car.

'I have insurance. I have insurance. I have insurance.' It was supposed to be her mantra. Saying things three times helped, only it didn't help enough. She put her head on the steering wheel and felt a wash of exhaustion so profound she felt like she was about to melt.

His car was trashed.

He climbed from the driver's seat and stared at his beloved Morgan in disbelief. The Morgan was low slung, gorgeous—and fragile. He'd parked her right in the centre of the bay to avoid the normal perils of parking lots—people opening doors and scratching his paintwork.

But the offending wagon had a bull bar attached and it hadn't just scratched his paintwork. While the wagon looked to be almost unscathed, the passenger-side panels of the Morgan had been sheared off completely.

He loved this baby. He'd bought her five years ago, a post-marriage toy to make him feel better about the world. He'd cherished her, spent a small fortune on her and then put her into very expensive storage while he'd been overseas.

His qualms about returning to Australia had been tempered by his joy on being reunited with Betsy. But now…some idiot with a huge lump of a wagon—and a bull bar…

'What the hell did you think you were doing?' He couldn't see the driver of the wagon yet, but he was venting his spleen on the wagon itself. Of all the ugly, lumbering excuses for a car...

And it was intact. Yeah, it'd have a few extra scratches but there were scratches all over it already. It was a battered, dilapidated brute and the driver'd be able to keep driving like the crash had never happened.

He wanted to kick it. Of all the stupid, careless...

Um...why hadn't the driver moved?

And suddenly medical mode kicked in, overriding rage. Maybe the driver had had a heart attack. A faint. Maybe this was a medical incident rather than sheer stupidity. He took a deep breath, switching roles in an instant. Infuriated driver became doctor. The wagon's driver's door was jammed hard against where his passenger door used to be, so he headed for its passenger side.

The wagon's engine died. Someone was alive in there, then. Good. Or sort of good.

He hauled the door open and he hadn't quite managed the transition. Rage was still paramount.

'You'd better be having a heart attack.' It was

impossible to keep the fury from his voice. 'You'd better have a really good excuse as to why you ploughed this heap of scrap metal into my car! You want to get out and explain?'

No!

Things were already appalling—but things just got a whole lot worse.

This was a voice she knew. A voice from her past.

Surely not.

She *had* to be imagining it, she decided, but she wasn't opening her eyes. If it really was...

It couldn't be. She was tired, she was frantically worried about Gretta, she was late and she'd just crashed her car. No wonder she was hearing things.

'You're going to have to open your eyes and face things.' She said it to herself, under her breath. Then she repeated it in her head twice more but her three-times mantra still didn't seem to be working.

The silence outside the car was ominous. Toe-tappingly threatening.

Maybe it'd go away if she just stayed...

'Hey, are you okay?' The gravelly voice, angry at first, was now concerned.

But it was the same voice and this wasn't her imagination. This was horrendously, appallingly real.

Voices could be the same, she told herself, feeling herself veering towards hysteria. There had to be more than one voice in the world that sounded like his.

She'd stay just one moment longer with her eyes closed.

Her passenger door opened and someone slid inside. Large. Male.

Him.

His hand landed on hers on the steering wheel. 'Miss? Are you hurt? Can I help?' And as the anger in his voice gave way to caring she knew, unmistakably, who this was.

Oliver. The man she'd loved with all her heart. The man who'd walked away five years ago to give her the chance of a new life.

So many emotions were slamming through her head...anger, bewilderment, grief... She'd had five years to move on but, crazy or not, this man still felt a part of her.

She'd crashed his car. He was right here.

There was no help for it. She took a deep, deep breath. She braced herself.

She raised her head, and she turned to face her husband.

Emily.

He was seeing her but his mind wasn't taking her in. Emily!

For one wild moment he thought he must be mistaken. This was a different woman, older, a bit...worn round the edges. Weary? Faded jeans and stained windcheater. Unkempt curls.

But still Emily.

His wife? She still was, he thought stupidly. His Em.

But she wasn't his Em. He'd walked away five years ago. He'd left her to her new life, and she had nothing to do with him.

Except she was here. She was staring up at him, her eyes reflecting his disbelief. Horror?

Shock held him rigid.

She'd wrecked his car. He loved this car. He should be feeling...

No. There was no *should*, or if there was he hadn't read that particular handbook.

Should he feel grief? Should he feel guilt?

He felt neither. All he felt was numb.

She'd had a minute's warning. He'd had none.

'Em?' He looked…incredulous. He looked more shocked than she was—bewildered beyond words.

What were you supposed to say to a husband you hadn't seen or spoken to for five years? There was no handbook for this.

'H-hi?' she managed.

'You've just crashed my car,' he said, stupidly.

'You were supposed to be a bike.' Okay, maybe that was just as stupid. This conversation was going exactly nowhere. They'd established, what, that he wasn't a bike?

He was her husband—and he was right beside her. Looking completely dumbfounded.

'You have a milk stain on your shoulder.'

That would be the first thing he'd notice, she thought. Her uniform was in her bag. She never put it on at home—her chances of getting out of the house clean were about zero—so she was still wearing jeans and the baggy windcheater she'd worn at breakfast.

Gretta had had a milky drink before being ill. Em had picked her up and cuddled her before she'd left.

Strangely, the stain left her feeling exposed. She didn't want this man to see...her.

'There are child seats in your wagon.'

He still sounded incredulous. Milk stains? Family wagon? He'd be seeing a very different woman from the one he'd seen five years ago.

But he looked...just the same. Same tall, lean, gorgeous. Same deep brown eyes that crinkled at the edges when he smiled, and Oliver smiled a lot. Same wide mouth and strong bone structure. Same dark, wavy hair, close cropped to try and get rid of the curl, only that never worked. It was so thick. She remembered running her fingers through that hair...

Um, no. Not appropriate. Regardless of formalities, this was her husband. Or ex-husband? They hadn't bothered with divorce yet but she'd moved on.

She'd just crashed his car.

'You're using Harry's car park,' she said, pointing accusingly at…um…one slightly bent sports car. It was beautiful—at least some of it still was. An open sports car. Vintage. It wasn't the sort of car that you might be able to pop down to the car parts place in your lunch hour and buy a new panel.

He'd always loved cars. She remembered the day they'd sold his last sports car.

His last? No. Who knew how many cars he'd been through since? Anyway, she remembered the day they'd sold the sleek little roadster both of them had loved, trading it in for a family wagon. Smaller than this but just as sensible. They'd gone straight from the car showroom to the nursery suppliers, and had had the baby seat fitted there and then.

She'd been six months pregnant. They'd driven home with identical smug looks on their faces.

He'd wanted a family as much as she had. Or she'd thought he did. What had happened then had proved she hadn't known him at all.

'I've been allocated this car park,' he was saying, and she had to force herself back to here, to now. 'Level Five, Bay Eleven. That's mine.'

'You're visiting?'

'I'm employed here, as of today.'

'You can't be.'

He didn't reply. He climbed out of the wagon, dug his hands deep in his pockets, glanced back at his wreck of a car and looked at her again.

'Why can't I, Em?' The wreck of the car faded to secondary importance. This was suddenly all about them.

'Because I work here.'

'It's the most specialised neonatal service in Melbourne. You know that's what I do.'

'You went to the States.' She felt numb. Stupid. Out of control. She'd been sure her ex-husband had been on the other side of world. She didn't want him to be here.

'I did specialist training in in-utero surgery in the States.' This was a dumb conversation. He was out of the car, leaning back on one of the concrete columns, watching her as she clung to the steering wheel like she was drowning. 'I've accepted a job back here. And before you say anything, no, I didn't know you were working here. I thought you were still at Hemmingway Private. I knew when I came back that there was a chance we might meet, but Melbourne's a big place. I'm not stalking you.'

'I never meant…'

'No?'

'No,' she managed. 'And I'm sorry I crashed into your car.'

Finally things were starting to return to normal. Like her heart rate. Her pulse had gone through the roof when the cars had hit. She'd been subconsciously trying to get it down, practising the deep-breathing techniques she used when she was pacing the floor with Gretta, frightened for herself, frightened for the future. The techniques came to her aid instinctively now when she was frightened. Or discombobulated.

Discombobulated was how she felt, she conceded. Stalking? That sounded as if he thought she might be frightened of him, and she'd never been frightened of Oliver.

'Can we exchange details?' she managed, trying desperately to sound normal. Like this was a chance meeting of old acquaintances, but they needed to talk about car insurance. 'Oliver, it's really nice to see you again…' Was it? Um, no, but it sounded the right thing to say. 'But I'm late as it is.'

'Which was why you crashed.'

'Okay, it was my fault,' she snapped. 'But, believe it or not, there are extenuating circumstances. That's not your business.' She clambered out of the car and dug for her licence in her shabby holdall. She pulled out two disposable diapers and a packet of baby wipes before she found her purse, and she was so flustered she dropped them. Oliver gathered them without a word, and handed them back. She flushed and handed him her licence instead.

He took it wordlessly, and studied it.

'You still call yourself Emily Evans?'

'You know we haven't divorced. That's irrelevant. You're supposed to take down my address.'

'You're living at your mother's house?'

'I am.' She grabbed her licence back. 'Finished?'

'Aren't you supposed to take mine?'

'You can sue me. I can't sue you. We both know the fault was mine. If you're working here then I'll send you my insurance details via interdepartmental memo. I don't carry them with me.'

'You seem to carry everything else.' Once more

he was looking into the car, taking in the jumble of kids' paraphernalia that filled it.

'I do, don't I?' she said, as cordially as she could manage. 'Oliver, it's good to see you again. I'm sorry I wrecked your car but I'm running really, really late.'

'You never run late.' He was right: punctuality used to be her god.

'I'm not the Emily you used to know,' she managed. 'I'm a whole lot different but this isn't the time or the place to discuss it.' She looked again at his car and winced. She really had made an appalling mess. 'You want me to organise some sort of tow?'

'Your car's hardly dented. I'll handle mine.'

'I'm...sorry.' She took a deep breath. 'Oliver, I really am sorry but I really do need to go. If there's nothing I can do...'

He was peering into her wagon. 'I doubt your lock's still working,' he told her. 'Once my car's towed free...'

'Locks are the least of my worries.' She slung her bag over her shoulder, knowing she had to move. She knew Isla was short-staffed this morning and the night staff would be aching to leave.

'Look at the stains,' she told him. 'No villain in their right mind would steal my wagon and, right now, I don't have time to care. I'm sorry to leave you with this mess, Oliver, but I need to go. Welcome to Victoria Hospital. See you around.'

CHAPTER TWO

RUBY DOWELL WAS seventeen years old, twenty-two weeks pregnant and terrified. She was Oliver's first patient at the Victoria.

She was also the reason he'd started so soon. He'd been recruited to replace Harry Eichmann, an obstetrician with an interest in in-utero procedures. Oliver had started the same way, but for him in-utero surgery was more than a side interest. For the last five years he'd been based in the States but he'd travelled the world learning the latest techniques.

The phone call he'd had from Charles Delamere, Victoria's CEO, had been persuasive, to say the least. 'Harry's following a girlfriend to Europe. There's no one here with your expertise and there's more and more demand.

'It's time you came home. Oliver, right now we have a kid here with a twenty-one-week foetus, and her scans are showing spina bifida. Heinz

Zigler, our paediatric neurologist, says the operation has to be done now. He can do the spinal stuff but he doesn't have the skills to stop the foetus aborting. Oliver, there are more and more of these cases, and we're offering you a full-time job. If you get here fast, we might save this kid shunts, possible brain damage, a life with limited movement below the waist. Short term, I want you to fight to give this kid a happy ending. Long term we're happy to fund your research. We'll cover the costs of whatever extra training you want, any staff you need. We want the best, Oliver, and we're prepared to pay, but we want you now.'

The offer had been great, but he'd had serious reservations about returning to Melbourne. He'd walked away from his marriage five years ago, and he'd thought he'd stay away. Em had deserved a new life, a chance to start again with someone who'd give her what she needed.

And it seemed his decision had been justified. Seeing her this morning, driving a family wagon, with milk stains on her shoulder, with every sign of being a frazzled young working mum, he'd thought…

Actually, he hadn't thought. The sight had

knocked him sideways and he was still knocked sideways. But he needed to focus on something other than his marriage. After a brief introduction with Charles, he was in the examination room with Ruby Dowell. Teenage mother, pregnant with a baby with spina bifida.

'At twenty-two weeks we need to get on with this fast,' Charles had told him. 'There's such a short window for meaningful intervention.'

Ruby was lying on the examination couch in a cubicle in the antenatal clinic and, as with all his patients, he took a moment at the start to assess the whole package. Her notes said she was seventeen. She'd been attending clinics in the Victoria's Teenage Mums-To-Be programme. When the spina bifida had been detected on the scans she'd been offered termination but had declined, although the notes said she intended to give the baby up for adoption after birth. Right now she was dressed in shorts and an oversized T-shirt. Her mouse-blonde, shoulder-length hair was in need of a wash and a good cut. Apart from the bump of her pregnancy she was waif thin, and her eyes were red-rimmed and wide with fear.

She looked like a wild creature trapped in a

cage, he thought. Hell, why was she alone? Her notes said she was a single mum, but she should have her mother with her, or a sister, or at least a friend.

It was unthinkable that such a kid was alone. Charles had said that Isla, his daughter and also the Victoria's head midwife, was in charge of the Teenage Mums-To-Be programme. Why hadn't she organised to be here, or at least sent a midwife in her place?

But now wasn't the time to head to the nurses' station and blast the powers that be for leaving her like this. Now was the time for reassurance.

'Hey,' he said, walking into the cubicle but deliberately leaving the screens open. He didn't need to do a physical examination yet, and he didn't want that trapped look to stay a moment longer. 'I'm the baby surgeon, Oliver Evans. I'm an obstetrician who's specially trained in operating on babies when they're still needing to stay inside their mums. And you're Ruby Dowell?'

He hauled a chair up to the bedside and summoned his best reassuring manner. 'Ruby, I'm here to get to know you, that's all. Nothing's happening right now. I'm just here to talk.'

But the terrified look stayed. She actually cringed back on the bed, fear radiating off her in waves. 'I'm...I'm scared of operations,' she stuttered. 'I don't want to be here.'

But then the screen was pulled back still further. A woman in nursing uniform, baggy tunic over loose pants, was fastening the screen so Ruby could see the nurses' station at the end of the corridor.

Emily. His wife.

His ex-wife? She'd never asked for a divorce but it had been simply a matter of signing the papers, any time these last five years.

'I'm scared of operations, too,' Em said, matter-of-factly, as if she'd been involved in the conversation from the start. 'I think everyone is. But Dr Evans here is the best baby surgeon in the known universe, I promise. I've known him for ever. If it was my baby there'd be no one else I'd want. Dr Evans is great, Ruby. He's kind, he's skilled and he'll give your baby the best chance of survival she can possibly have.'

'But I told you...I don't want her.' Ruby was sobbing now, swiping away tears with the back of her hand. 'My mum said I should have had an abortion. She would have paid. I don't know why I didn't. And now you're operating on a baby I don't even want. I just want you all to go away.'

In-utero surgery was fraught at the best of times. It was full of potential dangers for both mother and baby. To operate on a mother who didn't want her baby to survive…

He didn't know where to start—but he didn't need to, because Em simply walked forward, tugged the girl into her arms and held her.

Ruby stiffened. She held herself rigid, but Em's fingers stroked her hair.

'Hey, it's okay, Ruby. We all know how hard this is. Pregnancy's the pits. You feel so on your own, and you're especially on your own. You decided not to go ahead with an abortion, going against what your family wanted you to do. That took courage, but there's only so much courage a girl can be expected to show. That's why Isla's been helping you and it's why I'm here now. I'm *your* midwife, Ruby. I'll be with you every step of the way. All the decisions will be yours but I'm right with you. Right now, if you want Dr Evans to go away and come back later, he will. Just say the word.'

She met Oliver's gaze over Ruby's shoulder and her message was unmistakable. Back me up.

So Em was this girl's midwife? Then where the hell had she been when he'd walked in?

Coping with her crashed car, that's where, and then changing out of her mum clothes into nursing gear. Still, surely she could have made it earlier.

'We've had a drama with a prem birth I had to help with,' she said, as if he'd voiced his question out loud. She was still holding, still hugging, as Ruby's sobs went on. 'That's why I'm late, Ruby, and I'm sorry. I wanted to be here when you arrived. But I'm here now, and if you decide to proceed with this operation then you're my number one priority. Do you need some tissues? Dr Evans, hand me some tissues.'

'You helped with an earlier birth?' he asked, before he could help himself, and she had the temerity to glare at him.

'Yep. I had to step in and help the moment I hit the wards. Plus I crashed my car this morning. I crashed my wagon, Ruby, and guess whose gorgeous car I drove into? None other than Dr Evans.

It's his first day on the job and I hit him. It's a wonder he hasn't tossed me out of the room already.'

And Ruby's sobs hiccupped to a halt. She pulled back and looked at Em, then turned and stared at Oliver.

'She hit your car?'

'Yes,' he said. He wouldn't normally impart personal information to a patient but he guessed what Em was doing, and he could only agree. What Ruby needed was space to settle. He could help with that—even though he had to get personal to give it to her.

'I have a sixty-four Morgan Plus-4 sports car,' he said, mournfully, like the end of the world was nigh, which was about how he'd felt when he'd seen the damage—before he'd realised the driver of the other car had been Em. 'It's two-tone burgundy with black interior, a gorgeous two-seater. It's fitted with super sports upgrades, including twin Weber carbs, a Derrington header and a bonnet scoop. It also has chrome wire wheels, a badge bar with twin Lucas fog lamps and a tonneau cover. Oh, and it's retrofitted with overdrive transmission. Now it's also fitted with one smashed side—courtesy of your midwife.'

'Yikes,' Em said, but she didn't sound in the least subdued. 'Twin Weber carbs and a Derrington header, hey? Did I damage all that?'

'And if you knew how long it took to get those fog lamps...'

'Whoops. Sorry. But you scratched my car, too.' But Em was talking at Ruby rather than at him and she still sounded cheerful. Chirpy even.

'Scratched...' he muttered, and she grinned.

'That's okay. I forgive you. And they're cars. They're just things. That's what insurance is for. Whereas babies aren't things at all,' Em continued, leading seamlessly back to the reason they were all there. 'Ruby, your little girl is a person, not a thing, and she's far, far more precious. You made the decision to go ahead with this pregnancy. You made the decision early not to choose abortion and you chose it again when the scan showed spina bifida. But you've been telling me you think you might have her adopted when she's born...'

'I can't...deal with it.'

'You don't have to deal with it,' Em said soundly.

'There are lots of parents out there who'll give their eye teeth to have a baby like yours to love. That's right, isn't it, Dr Evans?'

'I… Yes.' But her words were like a punch in the gut. That last night… He'd tried to make her see one last time. *Em, I can't. I know adoption's the only way, but I can't do it. I can't guarantee to love a child who's not our own.*

'It will be our own.'

'Em, no.'

It had been their last conversation. He'd turned and walked away from the only woman he'd ever loved and it had nearly killed him. But she'd deserved the family she'd wanted so much. He'd had to give her that chance, and from the evidence he'd seen today, she'd taken it.

But now wasn't about him. It was all about Ruby. The kid's terror had been put aside. He had to take advantage of it.

Which meant putting thoughts of Em aside. Putting aside the knowledge that his wife, his ex-wife, presumably—did you need to formally sign papers to accept a marriage was over?—was in the same room.

'Ruby, you created this little girl,' he said, as

Em continued to hold her. 'You can have her adopted at birth, but until then you need to look after her. And the staff here have already explained to you—to look after her means an operation now.'

'But why?' Ruby demanded, suddenly belligerent. 'I don't understand. The kid's got spina bifida—Dr Zigler showed me on the scans. What difference does it make whether you operate now or operate when it's born?'

There was fear behind the question. Oliver recognised it. He'd done many in-utero procedures by now, and sometimes one of the hardest things was having the mum understand that the tiny child inside her was an independent being already. Something totally separate from her. This was a child who could be shifted in her uterus, who even at twenty-two weeks could cope with complex surgery and then be resettled, because, no matter how amazing the technology, the womb was still the safest place for her to be.

'Ruby, you know your baby has spina bifida,' he said now, gently. Em still had her arm around the girl. He was talking to them both, as he'd normally talk to a woman and her partner, or a woman and her mum or support person. Em had slid naturally into that role. A good midwife sometimes had to, he thought, and Em had always been brilliant at her job. Efficient, kind, skilled and empathic. He'd worked with her once and he'd loved it.

It was totally disconcerting to be working with her again, but he needed to focus on Ruby.

'You know we've picked up the spina bifida on the ultrasound,' Oliver said matter-of-factly, trying to take the emotion out of the situation. 'You've seen it?'

'It just looked blurry. I couldn't figure it out.'

So she didn't understand. 'Heinz Zigler's a great paediatric neurologist,' Charles had told him. 'He's technically brilliant, but communication's not his strong suit. He'll do the spinal surgery but everything else—including explanations to the mum—we're leaving to you.'

So now he needed to explain from the ground up. 'The scans do look blurry,' he admitted. 'I have trouble reading them myself. Fine detail like the nerve exposure around vertebrae needs incredibly specialised knowledge to see, but the radiologists here are superb. They've double-checked each other's work, and Dr Zigler agrees. Everyone's sure. But would you like me to explain what I think is happening? I don't talk in fine detail, Ruby. I just see the overview. That's actually what I do, total patient care, looking after you as well as your baby. I'm an obstetrician and a surgeon who specialises in looking after mums and bubs if bub needs an operation before it's time for her to be born.'

Silence. Ruby cast him a scared look and subsided. He waited, while Ruby pulled herself together a bit more, while Em handed her a wad of tissues, while both women readied themselves to front what was coming.

'Heinz says he told you the fine detail,' he said at last, when he thought Ruby was as ready as she was going to be. 'But here's the broad outline. The bones of your baby's spine—the vertebrae—haven't formed properly to protect your baby's spinal cord. The spinal cord holds the nerves that control your baby's movements. Because those nerves run right through the body, if the cord gets damaged then long term, your baby might not be able to walk. She might not have control of her bladder and bowel. If she has a severe problem she can also end up with a build-up of fluid in her brain. Then she'll need a shunt, all her life, to drain the excess fluid and relieve pressure.'

Ruby was crying again now, but not sobbing. Em's arm was around her, holding her close, but Ruby's attention was held. Her distress was taking second place to her need to know, and she seemed to be taking it in.

'So,' she whispered. 'So?'

'So the good thing is,' he said, still gently, 'that many problems of spina bifida aren't directly caused by the spina bifida itself. Doctors cleverer than me, like Heinz—did you know he's top in his field in research?—have worked out that the exposure of the spinal cord to the normal fluid in your womb, the amniotic fluid, is what progressively destroys the exposed nerves during pregnancy. If we can operate now, really early, and cover the exposed cord, then we prevent much of the damage. Your baby's much more likely to be able to live a normal, happy life.'

'But not with me,' Ruby whispered.

That was another issue altogether. Adoption. This was a single mum, a teenager, facing a life apart from the baby she was carrying.

'You haven't decided definitely on adoption,' Em murmured, and the girl shook her head.

'I can't think...'

'And you don't need to think.' Em's hold on her tightened. 'There's too much happening now for you to think past what you need to face right now. But, Ruby, regardless of what you decide to do when your baby's born, regardless of whether you decide you can care for her yourself or if you want to give her to parents who need a baby to love, she'll still be your daughter. You have the choice now to make a huge difference in your daughter's life.'

'You're...sure she has to have this operation?' Ruby whispered. 'I mean...really sure?'

'We're sure,' Oliver told her, suddenly immensely grateful for Em's presence. Without Em he doubted whether he'd have been able to get past the fear. 'But the operation's not without risks.' He had to say that. There was no way he could let this kid agree to surgery without warning her. 'Ruby, there are risks to you and risks to your baby. I believe those risks are small but they're still there.'

'But...I will make a difference.'

'Heinz tells me that because the spinal cord exposure is relatively high and very obvious on the ultrasound, then if we leave the operation undone, your daughter will probably spend her life in a wheelchair,' he said bluntly. 'And with the amount of exposure…there will be fluid build-up in the brain. She'll need a shunt and there may even be brain damage.'

'That's why Dr Evans has arrived here so fast,' Em went on smoothly. 'We haven't had a specialist in-utero surgeon on staff, but when we saw your ultrasound Dr Zigler knew we had to get the best obstetrician here as fast as we could. That's who Dr Evans is. The best. So now it's up to you, Ruby, love. Will you let us operate on your baby?'

'Heinz and I can close the gap over the cord,' Oliver told her. 'There's probably already a little damage done, but it's so early that damage should be minimal. What we'll do is put you to sleep, cut the smallest incision in your tummy as possible—you'll be left with a scar but I'm very neat.' He grinned at the girl, knowing a bit of pseudo modesty often worked, and he got a shaky smile in return. 'Then we'll gently turn your baby over where she's lying—with luck we won't have to take her out. Once her back is exposed Heinz will check everything, tweak things to where they should be, then we'll close the gap over her spinal cord. We'll settle her back down again and tuck her in, stitch you up and leave you both to get on with your pregnancy. You'll need to stay in hospital for about a week, maybe a bit longer, until we're sure we haven't pressured bub into coming early, but then everything should proceed as normal.'

'And she won't have to be in a wheelchair?'

'Ruby, we can't make any promises.' He caught her hand and held it. Em was still hugging her, and Oliver thought, not for the first time, Em was a wonderful midwife. She knew when to intervene and she knew when to shut up. She also exuded a quiet calm that was a tranquilliser all by itself.

He'd met her ten years ago. He'd been a barely qualified doctor, she'd been a student nurse, but already the confidence she'd engendered in the patients he'd worked with had been impressive. He'd seen her with some terrified teenage mums.

There was no nurse he'd rather have by his side and by the time they'd dated twice he'd known there was no woman he'd rather have with him for ever. Their attraction had been instant, their marriage inevitable.

It was only babies...or lack of babies...that had driven them apart.

The night their son had been stillborn had been the worst night of his life. He'd watched Em's face contort with an anguish so deep it had seemed endless, and there had been nothing he could do to stop it. He'd been unable to help her. He'd been unable to reach her.

But it was hardly the time to be thinking of that now. It was hardly the time to be thinking of it ever. After five years, they'd moved on.

'I can't make any promises,' he repeated, hauling himself back to the here and now, to the needs of the teenage kid in front of him. 'The procedure Heinz and I are trained to perform usually has an excellent outcome but there are exceptions. I won't hide that from you, Ruby. There are risks. There's a chance of infection, for you as well as your baby. We'll take every care in the world...'

'But no guarantees.'

'No guarantees,' he agreed. 'So it's up to you. This is your daughter, Ruby. It's up to you to make the choice.'

'I'm too young to have a daughter.' It was a wail and Em's arm tightened around her.

'That's where I come in,' she said solidly, a blanket of comfort and reassurance. 'You want advice, I'm full of advice. You want a hug, that's what I'm here for, too.'

'You can't be here with me all the time.'

'I can't,' Em agreed. 'I have my own son and daughter to look after. But I'm here every day during the week, and if I'm needed, I can come in at other times. My mum lives with me so I can usually drop everything and come. I don't do that for all my mums, but I'll try for you.'

'Why?' Ruby demanded, suspicious.

'Because you're special,' she said soundly. 'Isn't that right, Dr Evans? You're one special woman, and you're about to have one special daughter.'

But Oliver was hardly listening. Somehow he managed to make a grunt of acquiescence but his mind felt like it was exploding.

I have my own son and daughter to look after.

Somehow…a part of his brain had hoped—assumed?—that she'd stayed…as Em. The Em he'd left five years ago.

She hadn't. She'd moved on. She was a different woman.

I have my own son and daughter to look after...

'What do you think, Ruby?' Em was saying gently. 'Do you want to go ahead with the operation? Do you want time to think about it?'

'I don't have a choice,' Ruby whispered. 'My baby... It's the best thing...'

It was. Oliver watched Ruby's hand drop to cover the faint bulge of her tummy, the instinctive gesture of protection that was as old as time itself.

And the gesture brought back the wedge that had been driven so deep within his marriage that it had finished it. Em had wanted to adopt, and he'd known he couldn't love like parents were supposed to love. He was right, he thought bleakly. He'd always been right. What was between Ruby and her baby was what her baby needed. Ruby was this baby's mum. Adoption was great if there was no choice, but how could an adoptive parent ever love a child as much as this?

He knew he couldn't and that knowledge had torn his marriage apart.

But Em was watching him now, with those eyes

he'd once thought he could drown in. He'd loved her so much, and yet he'd walked away.

And she'd walked, as well.

I have my own son and daughter to look after.

It was nothing to do with him. He'd made his choice five years ago, and Em had obviously made choices, too.

He needed to know what those choices had been.

But now wasn't the time or the place to ask. All he could do was turn his attention back to Ruby, reassure her as much as possible and then set about working out times and details of the forthcoming surgery.

As they finished, a woman who introduced herself as one of the hospital social workers arrived. It seemed Ruby needed help with housing—as well as everything else, she'd been kicked out of her parents' house. She was staying in a boarding house near the hospital but she wouldn't be able to stay there when the baby was born.

There'd be more talk of adoption. More talk of options.

Ruby's surgery was scheduled for the day after tomorrow, but for now he was redundant. He was free to head to the next mum Charles had asked him to see.

He left, but his head was spinning.

Em was still sitting on the bed, still hugging Ruby. *I have my own son and daughter to look after.*

Whatever she'd done, it had been her choice. He'd walked away so she'd have that choice.

Why did it hurt so much that she'd taken it?

CHAPTER THREE

EM GOT ON with her day, too.

One of the wonderful things about being a midwife was that it took all her care, all her attention. She had little head-space for anything else. What was the saying? Find a job you love and you'll never have to work again? She'd felt that the first time she'd helped deliver a baby and she'd never looked back.

She sometimes…okay, she often…felt guilty about working when her mum was home with the kids, but the decision to foster had been a shared one. Her mum loved Gretta and Toby as much as she did. They had the big old house, but they needed Em's salary to keep them going.

Sometimes when Em got home her mother was more tired than she was, but whenever she protested she was cut off at the pass.

'So which baby are we giving back? Don't be ridiculous, Em. We can do this.'

They could, and knowing the kids were at home, waiting...it felt great, Em thought as she hauled off her uniform at the end of her shift and tugged on her civvies. Right, supermarket, pharmacy— Gretta's medications were running low—then home. She'd rung her mum at lunchtime and Adrianna had been reassuring. 'She's looking much better.' But, still, there was no way she was risking running out of Gretta's drugs.

'Big day?' Sophia Toulson, one of the more recent arrivals to the Victoria's midwifery staff, was hauling her uniform off, too, but instead of pulling on sensible clothes like Em's—yikes, where had that milk stain come from?—she was putting on clothes that said she was heading out clubbing or to a bar—to a life Em had left behind years ago.

Not that she missed it—much. Though there were times...

'It has been a big day,' she agreed, thinking of the night to come. Em had had three sleepless nights in a row. Gretta needed to be checked all the time. What she'd give for a solid eight-hour sleep...

'But have you met the new obstetrician? You must have—he's been fast-tracked here to operate on your Ruby. Em, he's gorgeous. No wedding ring, either. Not that that tells you anything with surgeons—they hardly ever wear them. It's not fair. Just because rings can hold infection it gives them carte blanche to disguise their marital state. But he's come from the States and fast, so that hints at single status. Em, you'll be working with him. How about giving it a shot?'

Yeah, right. Propositioning Oliver? If Sophia only knew... But somehow she managed to grimace as if this conversation were completely normal, an anonymous, gorgeous obstetrician arriving in the midst of midwives whose first love was their job, and whose second love was dissecting the love lives of those around them.

She turned to face the full-length mirror at the end of the change room. What she saw there made her grimace. Faded jeans, with a rip at the knee. Trainers with odd shoelaces. A windcheater with a milk stain running down the shoulder—why hadn't she noticed that before she'd left the house?

Her hair needed a cut. Oliver had loved her hair. She'd had it longer then and the dull brown had been shiny. It had bounced—she'd spent time with decent shampoo and conditioner, and she'd used a curling wand to give it body.

Now she bought her shampoo and conditioner in bulk at the discount store and her curling wand was rusting under the sink.

Oliver had never seen her like this—until today.

Sophia was suggesting she make a play for him?

'Can you see Oliver Evans with someone like me?' she asked incredulously. 'Sophia, get real.'

'You could try,' Sophia said, coming up behind her friend and staring over her shoulder at the reflection. 'Em, you're really pretty. With a bit of effort…'

'All my effort goes into the kids.'

'You're burying yourself.'

'I'm giving them a chance.' She glanced at her watch and grimaced again. 'Ouch. I need to go. Have a great time tonight.'

'I wish I could say the same for you. Home with your mum and two kids…' She bit her lip and Em knew why. Sophia had the same problem she did—she'd barely worked with her for a month before she'd winkled out of her the reason for the gravity behind what somehow seemed a forced gaity.

Did all women who couldn't have children feel like this? Maybe they did, but Em's solution horrified Sophia.

'I love it,' she said soundly, even defiantly, because she did. Of course she did. 'And you have fun at… Where are you going?'

'The Rooftop Bar. Madeleine just happened to mention to your Dr Evans that we might be there.' She grinned and started searching her bag for her lipstick. 'If you're not interested…'

'He's all yours,' Em said tightly. 'Best of luck. The supermarket's waiting for me. Whoo-hoo, a fabulous night for both of us.'

'Right,' Sophia said dryly. 'Em, I wish…'

'Well, don't wish,' Em said, more sharply than she'd intended. 'Don't even think about it. This is the life I chose for myself, and I'm happy. Dr Oliver Evans might be at the bar and I guess that's the life he's chosen, too. We're all where we want to be, and we can't ask for more than that.'

Oliver's day wasn't supposed to be frantic. Weren't new staff supposed to have an orientation day, a shift where they spent the time acquainting themselves with ward and theatre staff, meeting everyone in the canteen, arranging stuff in their office? Not so much. Harry, it seemed, had left in a hurry. His lady had been enticing; he'd left without giving proper notice and the work had backed up.

Apart from that, Harry hadn't had specialist in-utero surgical training. It seemed that word of Oliver's arrival had flown around Melbourne before he arrived. He had three consultations lined up for the afternoon and more for the next day.

Ruby's case was probably the most complex. No, it *was* the most complex, he thought, mostly because the scans showing the extent of the problem had made him wince.

Plus she was alone. His next mum, Lucy, arrived with a support cast, husband, parents, an entourage of six. Her baby had a congenital heart malfunction. The little boy in utero was a twenty-four-weeker. He needed an aortic valvuloplasty—opening the aortic foetal heart valves to allow blood flow. It was one of the most common reasons for in-utero surgery, the one that Oliver was most comfortable with—as long as he had the backup of decent cardiac surgeons.

Oliver had already met Tristan Hamilton, the Victoria's neonatal cardiothoracic surgeon—in fact, they'd gone to university together. Tristan had backed up Charles's calls, pressuring him to come, and he had been one of the inducements. Tristan was incredibly skilled, and if he could work side by side with him, for this mum, things were likely to be fine.

But what seemed wrong was that Lucy and her little boy had huge family backup—and Ruby had no one.

But Ruby had Em.

That had to be compensation. Em would be terrific.

If indeed she was with her. She'd been running late that morning. She'd looked harassed, like she had one too many balls in the air.

She'd come flying into Ruby's room half an hour after she'd hit his car, burbling about an early delivery. Really? Or had she spent the half hour on the phone to her insurance people?

It was none of his business.

Still, it was a niggle…

Isla Delamere was the Victoria's head midwife—plus she was the daughter of the CEO. Apparently she'd also just become engaged to the hospital's neonatal intensive care specialist. Isla was not a person to mess with, he'd decided. He'd been introduced to her by Charles, and as he was about to leave he saw her again.

'You have how many in-utero procedures lined up for me?' he said, half joking. 'You guys believe in throwing me in at the deep end.'

'You just do the surgery,' she said, smiling. 'My midwives will keep everything running smoothly. I have the best team…'

'My midwife this morning was running late.' He shouldn't have said it. He knew it the moment he'd opened his mouth. The last thing he wanted was to get Em into trouble and this woman had power at her fingertips, but Isla didn't seem bothered.

'I'm sorry about that. We had three births within fifteen minutes of each other just as Em came on duty. I know her care of Ruby's a priority, but one of the births was prem, the mum was out of her tree, and there's no one better at calming a frantic mum than Em. I only used her for the final fifteen minutes but it made a difference. You did cope by yourself until then?'

She raised her beautifully formed eyebrows quizzically…head midwife wondering if surgeon could cope without a little assistance…

Right. He'd got his answer but now Isla thought he was a wimp. Great start.

'Some of the staff are going to the Rooftop Bar after work,' Isla told him. 'Have you been invited? You're welcome to join us.'

'Thanks but I have a problem to sort.'

'Your car?' She was still smiling and, he thought, that was just the sort of thing that hospital staff the world over enjoyed. Specialist's car being trashed, especially since most staff here could never afford to run a car like Betsy.

He loved that car and now she was a mess. But...

'Em's promised to sort it,' Isla told him. 'She's not the sort of woman to let her insurance lapse.'

'It's not the insurance...'

'And she's really sorry. She was stricken when she first came in this morning. She's been so busy all day I suspect she hadn't had time to apologise but—'

'Will she be at the bar now?'

'Em? Heavens, no. She has two kids waiting for her at home.'

'Two?'

'Gretta's four and Toby's two. They're special kids but, wow, they're demanding.'

'I guess...' And then he asked because he couldn't help himself. Had a miracle happened? *Gretta's four...* She must have moved like the wind. 'Her partner...' He knew there couldn't have been a marriage because there'd never been a divorce but...there must be someone. 'Is he a medic? Does she have help?'

But Isla's eyebrows hit her hairline. Her face closed, midwife protecting her own. 'I guess that's for you to ask Em if it's important for you to know,' she said shortly, clearing her desk, making signals she was out of there. Off to the Rooftop Bar to join her colleagues? 'She doesn't talk about her private life. Is there anything else you need?'

More information, he thought, and he'd bet Isla knew everything he wanted to know. But he couldn't push without opening a can of worms. Evans was a common name. Em had clearly not told anyone there was a connection.

Better to leave it that way, maybe.

'Thanks, no.'

'Goodnight, then. And good luck with the car. You might let Em know when you have it sorted. She's beating herself up over it. She's a great midwife and I don't like my midwives stressed. I'd appreciate it if you could fix it.'

'I'll try,' he said, but it was too late. Isla had gone.

He headed down to the car park. He hadn't been back to assess the damage during the day—he hadn't had time.

The park next to his was empty. Em was gone.

Her wagon had still been drivable. Her doors had been bent, but the wheels were still okay, whereas his… One of the wheels was far from okay and he wasn't driving anywhere. He stooped and examined it and thought of the hassle it had been to find the right parts for his little beauty. Where was he going to find another wheel rim? And the panels were a mess.

Strangely, it didn't upset him as much as he'd thought it might. He checked the damage elsewhere and knew he'd have to get her towed—actually, carried, as there was no way she could be towed like this. And then he'd go searching for the parts he needed.

He kind of liked searching the internet for car parts. It was something to do at three in the morning when he couldn't sleep.

Which was often.

He rounded the front of the car and there he saw a note in his windshield. Em?

Oliver, I really am sorry about this. I've put my hand up, it was all my fault, and I've told my insurance company to pay without arguing. I photocopied my driver's licence and my insurance company details—they're attached. One of the girls on the ward knows of a great repair place that specialises in vintage cars— the details are here, too. See you when you next see Ruby.

Em

It was all about the car. There was nothing personal at all.

Well, what did he expect? A *mea culpa* with extras? This was more than generous, admitting total culpability. Her insurance company would hate her. As well as that, she'd probably have to pay the first few hundred dollars, plus she'd lose her no-claim bonus.

He could afford it. Could she?

He re-read the note. What was he hoping for? Personal details?

Her driver's licence told him all he was going to get. Emily Louise Evans. She was still using his name, then. So…single mother? How? Had she gone ahead and adopted by herself? He checked again, making sure he was right—she was living at her mother's address.

He liked Adrianna. Or he had liked her. He hadn't seen his mother-in-law for years.

He could drop in…

Why?

'Because she shouldn't accept full responsibility,' he said out loud. 'If she's supporting kids…'

She'd said she'd already phoned her insurance company and confessed, but maybe he could reverse it. Maybe he could take some of the load.

The independent Em of five years ago would tell him to shove it.

Yeah? He thought back to the Em of five years ago, shattered, gutted, looking towards the future with a bleakness that broke his heart.

'If you won't do it with me then I'll do it alone. If you think I can go back to the life we led… I'm over nightclubs, Oliver. I'm over living just for me.'

'Isn't there an us in there?'

'I thought there was, but I thought we wanted a family. I hadn't realised it came with conditions.'

'Em, I can't.'

'So you're leaving?'

'You're not giving me any choice.'

'I guess I'm not. I'm sorry, Oliver.'

Five years…

Okay, their marriage was long over but somehow she still seemed…partly his responsibility. And the cost of this repair would make her insurance company's eyes water.

It behoved him…

'Just to see,' he told himself. He'd thought he'd drop in to visit Adrianna when he'd come to Melbourne anyway, to see how she was.

And talk to Adrianna about Em?

Yeah, but he was over it. He'd had a couple of relationships in the last five years, even if they had been fleeting. He'd moved on.

'So let's be practical,' he told himself, and hit his phone and organised a tow truck, and a hire car, and half an hour later he was on the freeway, heading to the suburb where his ex-mother-in-law lived. With his wife and her two children, and her new life without him.

* * *

'You hit who?'

'Oliver.' Em was feeding Toby, which was a messy joy. Toby was two years old and loved his dinner. Adrianna had made his favourite animal noodles in a tomato sauce. Toby was torn between inspecting every animal on his spoon and hoovering in the next three spoonfuls as if there was no tomorrow.

Adrianna was sitting by the big old fire stove, cuddling Gretta. The little girl's breathing was very laboured.

Soon...

No. It hurt like hot knives to have to think about it. Much better to concentrate on distractions, and Oliver was surely a distraction.

'He's working at the Victoria?'

'Yep. Starting today.'

'Oh, Em... Can you stay there?'

'I can't walk away. We need the money. Besides, it's the best midwifery job in Melbourne. I love working with Isla and her team.'

'So tell him to leave. You were there first.'

'I don't think you can tell a man like Oliver Evans to leave. Besides, the hospital needs him.

I read his CV on the internet during lunch break. His credentials are even more awesome than when I knew him. He's operating on Ruby's baby and there's no one better to do it.'

And that had Adrianna distracted. 'How is Ruby?'

Em wasn't supposed to bring work home. She wasn't supposed to talk about patients outside work, but Adrianna spent her days minding the kids so Em could work. Adrianna had to feel like she was a part of it, and in a way she was. If it wasn't for her mum, she'd never be able to do this.

This. Chaos. Animal noodles. Mess on the kitchen floor. Fuzzy, a dopey half-poodle, half something no one could guess at, was currently lurking under Toby's highchair on the off-chance the odd giraffe or elephant would drop from on high.

'Hey, it's all done.' There was a triumphant bang from the laundry and Mike appeared in the doorway, waving his spanner. 'That's that mother fixed. I'd defy any drop to leak anywhere now. Anything else I can do for you ladies?'

'Oh, Mike, that's fabulous. But I wish you'd let us pay—'

'You've got free plumbing for life,' Mike said fiercely. Mike was their big, burly, almost scary-looking next-door neighbour. His ginger hair was cropped to almost nothing. He wore his jeans a bit too low, he routinely ripped the sleeves out of his T-shirts because sleeves annoyed him, and in his spare time he built his body. If you met Mike on a dark night you might turn the other way. Fast.

Em had met Mike on a dark night. He'd crashed into their kitchen, banging the back door so hard it had broken.

'Em, the wife… My Katy… The baby… There's blood, oh, my God, there's blood… You're a mid-wife. Please…'

Katy had had a fast, fierce delivery of their third child, and she'd haemorrhaged. Mike had got home to find her in the laundry, her baby safely delivered, but she'd been bleeding out.

She'd stopped breathing twice before the ambulance had arrived. Em had got her back.

Mike and Katy were now the parents of three boys who promised to grow up looking just like their dad, and Mike was Em's slave for ever. He'd taken Em and her household under his wing, and a powerful wing it was. There were usually motorbikes parked outside Mike and Katy's place—multiple bikes—but no matter what the pressure of his family, his job or his biker mates, Mike dropped in every night—just to check.

Now, as Toby finished the last mouthful of his noodles, Mike hefted him out of his highchair and whirled him round and hugged him in a manner that made Em worry the noodles might come back up again. But Toby crowed in glee.

'Can I take him next door for a few minutes?' he asked. 'We've got a new swing, a double-seater. My boys'll be outside and Henry and Tobes'll look a treat on it. Give you a bit of peace with Gretta, like.'

He glanced at Gretta but he didn't say any more. What was happening was obvious. Gretta was more and more dependent on oxygen, but more and more it wasn't enough.

If Mike took Toby, Em could sit by the fire and cuddle Gretta while Adrianna put her feet up and watched the telly. Toby was already lighting up with excitement.

'That'd be great, Mike, thank you,' Em told him. 'I'll pop over and pick him up in an hour.'

'Bring Gretta with you,' Mike said. 'Give her a go on the swing. If she's up for it.'

But she wasn't up for it. They all knew it, and that knowledge hung over the house, a shadow edging closer.

Today Oliver's presence had pushed that shadow back a little, made Em's thoughts fly sideways, but, Oliver or not, the shadows were there to stay.

CHAPTER FOUR

THE LAST TIME Oliver had visited his ex-mother-in-law, her house had looked immaculate. Adrianna was devoted to her garden. At this time of year her roses had always looked glorious, her herbaceous borders had been clipped to perfect symmetry and her lawns had always been lush and green, courtesy of the tanks she'd installed specifically so she could be proud of her garden the year round.

Not now.

The grass on the lawn was a bit long and there were bare patches, spots where things had been left for a while. Where once an elegant table setting had stood under the shade of a Manchurian pear, there was now a sandpit and a paddling pool.

A beach ball lay on the front path. He had to push it aside to reach the front door.

It took him less than a minute to reach the door but by the time he had, the last conversation he'd had with Em had played itself out more than a dozen times in his head.

'Em, I can't adopt. I'm sorry, but I can't guarantee I can love kids who aren't my own.'

'They would be your own,' she'd said. She'd been emotional, distraught, but underneath she'd been sure. *'I want kids, Oliver. I want a family. There are children out there who need us. If we can't have our own...to not take them is selfish.'*

'To take them when we can't love them is selfish.'

'I can love them. I will.'

'But I can't.' He'd said it gently but inexorably, a truth he'd learned by fire.

'You're saying I need to do it alone?'

'Em, think about it,' he'd said fiercely. *'We love each other. We've gone through so much...'*

'I want a family.'

'Then I can't give it to you. If this is the route you're determined to take, then you'll need to find someone who can.'

He'd walked away, sure that when she'd settled she'd agree with him. After all, their love was absolute. But she'd never contacted him. She hadn't answered his calls.

Adrianna had spoken to him. 'Oliver, she's gutted. She knows your position. Please, leave her be to work things out for herself.'

It had gutted him, too, that she'd walked away from their marriage without a backward glance. And here was evidence that she'd moved on. She'd found herself the life she wanted—without him.

He reached the door, lifted his hand to the bell but as he did the door swung inwards.

The guy opening the door was about the same age as Oliver. Oliver was tall, but this guy was taller and he was big in every sense of the word. He was wearing jeans, a ripped T-shirt and big working boots. His hands were clean but there was grease on his forearms. And on his tatts.

He was holding a child, a little boy of about two. The child was African, Oliver guessed, Somalian maybe, as dark as night, with huge eyes. One side of his face was badly scarred. He was cradled in the guy's arms, but he was looking outwards, brightly interested in this new arrival into his world.

Another kid came flying through the gate behind Oliver, hurtling up the path towards them.

Another little boy. Four? Ginger-haired. He looked like the guy in front of him.

'Daddy, Daddy, it's my turn on the swing,' he yelled. 'Come and make them give me a turn.'

The guy scooped him up, as well, then stood, a kid tucked under each arm. He looked Oliver up and down, like a pit bull, bristling, assessing whether to attack.

'Life insurance?' he drawled. 'Funeral-home plans? Not interested, mate.'

'I'm here to see Emily.'

'She's not interested, either.'

He was still wearing his suit. Maybe he should have changed. Maybe a tatt or two was necessary to get into this new version of his mother-in-law's home.

'I'm a friend of Em's from the hospital.' Who was this guy? 'Can you tell her I'm here, please?'

'She's stuffed. She doesn't need visitors.' He was blocking the doorway, a great, belligerent bull of a man.

'Can you ask her?'

'She only has an hour at most with Gretta before the kid goes to sleep. You want to intrude on that?'

Who was Gretta? Who was this guy?

'Mike?' Thankfully it was Em, calling from inside the house. 'Who is it?'

'Guy who says he's a friend of yours.' Mike didn't take his eyes off Oliver. His meaning was clear—he didn't trust him an inch. 'Says he's from the hospital. Looks like an undertaker.'

'Mike?'

'Yeah?'

'It'll be Oliver,' she called, and Mike might be right about the 'stuffed' adjective, Oliver conceded. Her voice sounded past weariness.

'Oliver?'

'He's the guy I was married to.' *Was?*

'Your ex is an undertaker? Sheesh, Em...'

'He's not an undertaker. He's a surgeon.'

'That's one step before the undertaker.'

'Mike?'

'Yeah?'

'Let him in.'

Why didn't Em come to the door? But Mike gave him a last long stare and stepped aside.

'Right,' he called back to Em. 'But we're on the swings. One yell and I'll be here in seconds. Watch it, mate,' he growled at Oliver, as he pushed past him and headed down the veranda with his load of kids. 'You upset Em and you upset me—and you wouldn't want to do that. You upset Em and you'll be very, very sorry.'

He knew this house. He'd been here often with Em. He'd stayed here for weeks on end when, just after they were married, Em's dad had been diagnosed with inoperable lung cancer.

It had taken the combined skill of all of them—his medical input, Em's nursing skill and Adrianna's unfailing devotion—to keep Kev comfortable until the end, but at the funeral, as well as sadness there had also been a feeling that it had been the best death Kev could have asked for. Surrounded by his family, no pain, knowing he was loved...

'This is how I want us to go out when we have to,' Em had whispered to him at the graveside. 'Thank you for being here.'

Yeah, well, that was years ago and he hadn't been with her for a long time now. She was a different woman.

He walked into the kitchen and stopped dead.

Different woman? What an understatement.

She was sitting by Adrianna's old kitchen range,

settled in a faded rocker. Her hair was once more loose, her curls cascading to her shoulders. She had on that baggy windcheater and jeans and her feet were bare.

She was cuddling a child. A three- or four-year-old?

A sick child. There was an oxygen concentrator humming on the floor beside them. The child's face was buried in Em's shoulder, but Oliver could see the thin tube connected to the nasal cannula.

A child this small, needing oxygen… His heart lurched. This was no ordinary domestic scene. A child this sick…

The expression on Em's face…

Already he was focusing forward. Already he was feeling gutted for Em. She gave her heart…

Once upon a time she'd given it to him, and he'd hurt her. That she be hurt again…

This surely couldn't be her child.

And who was Mike?

He'd paused in the doorway and for some reason it took courage to step forward. He had no place in this tableau. He'd walked away five years ago so this woman could have the life she wanted, and he had no right to walk back into her life now.

But he wasn't walking into her life. He was here to talk to her about paying for the crash.

Right. His head could tell him that all it liked, but his gut was telling him something else entirely. Em... He'd loved her with all his heart.

He looked at her now, tired, vulnerable, holding a child who must be desperately ill, and all he wanted was to pick her up and carry her away from hurt.

From loving a child who wasn't hers?

Maybe she was hers. Maybe the in-vitro procedures had finally produced a successful outcome. But if this was her child...

His gut was still churning, and when she turned and gave him a tiny half-smile, a tired acknowledgement that he was there, a sort of welcome, the lurch became almost sickening.

'Ollie.'

No one had called him Ollie for five years. No one dared. He'd hated the diminutive—Brett, his sort of brother, had mocked him with it. *Get out of our lives, Pond Scum Ollie. You're a cuckoo. You don't belong here.*

Only Em had whispered it to him in the night, in his arms, when their loving had wrapped them in their own cocoon of bliss. Only Em's tongue had made it a blessing.

'Hey,' he said softly, crossing to where she sat, and, because he couldn't help himself, he touched her hair. Just lightly. He had no right, but he had to…touch.

It was probably a mistake. It hauled him into the intimate tableau. Em looked up at him and smiled, and it was no longer a half-smile. It was a smile of welcome. Acceptance.

A welcome home? It was no such thing. But it was a welcome to *her* home, to the home she'd created. Without him.

'Gretta, we have a visitor,' she murmured, and she turned slightly so the child in her arms could see if she wanted.

And she did. The little girl stirred and opened her eyes and Oliver's gut lurched all over again.

Isla had said Em had a two- and a four-year-old. This little one was older than two, but if she was four she was tiny. She was dressed in a fuzzy pink dressing gown that almost enveloped her.

She was a poppet of a child, with a mop of dark, straight hair, and with huge eyes, almost black.

Her lips were tinged blue. The oxygen wasn't enough, then.

She had Down's syndrome.

Oh, Em… What have you got yourself into?

But he couldn't say it. He hauled a kitchen chair up beside them both, and took Gretta's little hand in his.

'I'm pleased to meet you, Gretta.' He smiled at the little girl, giving her all his attention. 'I'm Oliver. I'm a friend of your…' And he couldn't go on.

'He's Mummy's friend,' Em finished for him, and there was that lurch again. 'He's the man in the picture next to Grandma and Grandpa.'

'Ollie,' the little girl whispered, and there was no outsider implication in that word. She was simply accepting him as part of whatever this household was.

There was a sudden woof from under the table, a scramble, another woof and a dog's head appeared on his knee. It was a great, boofy, curly brown head, attached to a body that was disproportionally small. It woofed again but its tail wagged like a flag in a gale.

'This is Fuzzy,' Em said, still smiling at him. His presence here didn't seem to be disconcerting her. It was as if he was simply an old friend, dropping by. To be welcomed and then given a farewell? 'Mike gave us Fuzzy to act as a watch-dog. He sort of does, but he's always a bit late on the scene.'

'Oliver!' And here was the last part of the tab-leau. Adrianna was standing in the door through to the lounge and her eyes weren't welcoming at all. 'What are you doing here?'

Here was the welcome he'd expected. Coldness and accusation...

'Mum...' Em said warningly, but Adrianna was never one who could be put off with a mere warn-ing.

'You hit Em's car.'

'Mum, I told you. I hit his.'

'Then he shouldn't have been parked where you could hit him. What are you doing here?'

'Offering to pay for the damage.'

Her eyes narrowed. 'Really?'

'Really.'

'Mum, it was my fault,' Em protested, but Adri-anna shook her head.

'It's your no-claim bonus that's at risk. Oliver's a specialist obstetric surgeon, and I'm betting he has no mortgage and no kids. He can afford it.'

'Mum, it's my debt.'

'You take on the world,' her mother muttered. 'Oliver owes you, big time. My advice is to take his money and run. Or rather take his money and say goodbye. Oliver, you broke my daughter's heart. I won't have you upsetting her all over again. Raking up old wounds...'

'He's not,' Em said, still gently, and Oliver was aware that her biggest priority was not Em or the emotions his presence must be causing, but rather on not upsetting the little girl in her arms. 'Mum, he's welcome. He's a friend and a colleague and he's here to do the honourable thing. Even if I won't let him. I can afford to pay, Oliver.'

'I won't let you,' he told her.

'I'll make you a cup of tea, then,' Adrianna said, slightly mollified. She humphed across to the kettle, made tea—and, yep, she remembered how he liked it. She plonked two mugs on the table, one for Em, one for him. Then she hoisted Fuzzy into one arm, took her own mug in the other hand and headed back to the sitting room. 'Semi-final of *Boss of My Kitchen*,' she said briefly over her shoulder. 'Shall the croquembouche disintegrate into a puddle? The tension's a killer. Nice to see you, Oliver—sort of—but don't you dare upset Em. Goodbye.'

And she disappeared, using a foot to shove the door closed behind her.

Her message couldn't be clearer. *My daughter wants me to be polite so I will be, but not one inch more than I must.*

He was left with Em, and the little girl in her arms. Sitting in Adrianna's kitchen.

It was a great kitchen.

He'd always loved this house, he thought, inconsequentially. Kevin and Adrianna had built it forty years ago, hoping for a huge family. They'd had four boys, and then the tail-ender, Emily. Adrianna's parents had moved in, as well, into a bungalow out the back. Em had said her childhood had been filled with her brothers and their mates, visiting relations, cousins, friends, anyone Adrianna's famous hospitality could drag in.

Oliver and Em had built a house closer to the hospital they both worked in. They'd built four bedrooms, as well, furnishing them with hope.

Hope hadn't happened. The IVF procedures had worn them down and Josh's death had been the final nail in the coffin of their marriage. He'd walked out and left it to her.

'You're not living in our house?' He'd signed

it over to her before going overseas, asking their lawyer to let her know.

'It's better here,' she said simply. 'My brothers are all overseas or interstate now, but I have Mum, and Mike and Katy nearby. The kids are happy here. I've leased our house out. When I emailed you, you said I could do what I like. I use half the rent to help with expenses here. The other half is in an interest-bearing deposit for you. I told you that in the email. You didn't answer.'

He hadn't. He'd blocked it out. The idea of strangers living in the gorgeous house he and Em had had built with such hopes...

'I couldn't live there,' Em said, conversationally. 'It doesn't have heart. Not like here. Not like home.'

Yeah, well, that was another kick in the guts, but he was over it by now. Or almost over it. He concentrated on his tea for a bit, while Em juggled Gretta and cannula and her mug of tea. He could offer to help but he knew he'd be knocked back.

She no longer needed him. This was her life now.

Gretta was watching him, her great brown eyes carefully assessing. Judging? Who knew? The IQs of kids with Down's syndrome covered an amazingly broad spectrum.

He touched the cannula lightly. 'Hey, Gretta,' he said softly. 'Why do you need this?'

'For breeving,' she lisped, but it was as if even saying the words was too much for her. She sank back against Em and her eyes half closed.

'Gretta has an atrioventricular septal defect,' Em said matter-of-factly, as if it was a perfectly normal thing for a kid to have. No problem at all.

But those three words told Oliver all he needed to know about the little girl's condition.

An atrioventricular septal defect… Common term—hole in the heart.

A large percentage of babies with Down's syndrome were born with congenital heart defects. The most common problem was atrioventricular septal defects, or holes in the heart. That this little one was at home with oxygen, with a cannula helping her breathe, told Oliver there was more than one hole. It must be inoperable.

And he had to ask.

'Em, is she yours?'

The words echoed around the kitchen, and as soon as they came out he knew it was the wrong thing to ask. The arms holding Gretta tightened, and so did the look on Em's face.

'Of course she's mine,' she whispered, but the friendliness was gone. 'Gretta's my daughter. Oliver, I think you should leave.'

'I meant—'

'You meant is she adopted?' Her face was still bleak. 'No, she's not adopted. I'm Gretta's foster-mum, but her birth mother has given all responsibility to me. That means I can love her as much as I want, and that's what I do. I love her and love her and love her. Gretta's my daughter, Oliver, in every sense of the word.'

'You have another...son?'

'You'll have met Toby on the way out with Mike, and he's my foster-child, too. He has spinal kyphoscoliosis. He's the bravest kid. I'm so proud of my kids. Mum's so proud of her grandkids.'

He got it. Or sort of. These were fostered kids. That's what Em had wanted him to share.

But that's what he'd been, he thought bleakly. Someone else's reject. Much as he approved of the idea in theory, in practice he knew it didn't work.

But what Em did was no longer his business, he

reminded himself. This was what she'd decided to do with her life. He had no business asking...

How could he not?

'Who's Mike?' he asked, and he hadn't known he was going to ask until he did.

'My lover?' Her lips twitched a little at the expression on his face. 'Can you see it? Nope, Mike's our next-door neighbour, our friend, our man about the house. He and Katy have three kids, we have two, and they mix and mingle at will. You like going to Katy's, don't you, Gretta?'

There was a faint nod from Gretta, and a smile.

And the medical part of Oliver was caught. If Gretta was responding now, as ill as she was, her IQ must be at the higher end of the Down's spectrum.

He watched Em hold her tight, and he thought, She's given her heart...

And he never could have. He'd never doubted Em's ability to adopt; it was only his reluctance... his fear...

'Is there anything I can do to help?' he found himself saying. 'Now that I'm here?'

'But you don't want to be here.' Em shifted a little, making herself more comfortable. 'You've moved on. At least, I hope you have. I'd have thought you'd have asked for a divorce, found a new partner and had kids by now. You wanted kids. What's stopping you?'

And there was a facer. He had wanted children, they both had, but after a stillbirth and so many attempts at IVF it had worn them—and their marriage—into the ground. Em had told him to leave.

No. She hadn't. She'd simply said she wanted to adopt a child, and that was a deal-breaker.

'I haven't found the right person,' he said, trying to make it sound flippant, but there was no way he could make anything about what had happened to them flippant. The last year or so of their marriage had been unswervingly grey. He looked at Em now and he thought some of the grey remained.

A lot of the grey?

He glanced around the kitchen, once sparkling and ordered, if a bit cluttered with Adrianna's bits and pieces from the past. But now it was all about the present. It was filled with the detritus of a day with kids—or a life with kids.

But this was what Em wanted. And he hadn't?

No, he thought fiercely. It had been what he'd

wanted more than anything, and that's why he'd walked away.

So why hadn't he found it?

There was the sound of feet pounding up the veranda, a perfunctory thump on the door and two little boys of about six and four burst in. They were followed by Mike, carrying the toddlers. The six-year-old was carrying a bunch of tattered kangaroo paws, flowers Oliver had seen in the next-door front garden. Tough as nails, Australian perennials, they hardly made good cut flowers but these were tied with a gaudy red bow and presented with pride.

'These are for Gran Adrianna,' the urchin said. And when she obviously wasn't in the kitchen, he headed through the living-room door and yelled for her. 'Gran? Gran Adrianna, we've got you a present. Mum says happy birthday. She was coming over to say it but she's got a cold and she says she wants to give you flowers for your birthday and not a cold.'

And Em turned white.

CHAPTER FIVE

EVERYONE ELSE WAS looking at the kid with the flowers, and then at Adrianna, who reappeared and stooped to give the kids a hug. Only Oliver saw the absolute mortification that crossed Em's face.

She'd forgotten, he thought. Of course she had. Even if she'd remembered this morning, after crashing her car, doing a huge day on the wards, then coming home to such a sick kid, forgetting was almost inevitable.

Think. Think! he told himself. He used to live in this town. Cake. St Kilda. Ackland Street. Cake heaven. It wasn't so far, and the shops there stayed open late.

'Are you guys staying for the cake?' he asked, glancing at his watch, his voice not rising, speaking like this was a pre-ordained plan. 'It'll be here in about twenty minutes. Em asked me to order it but it's running a bit late. Adrianna, is it okay if

I stay for the celebration? Em thought it might be okay, but if you'd rather I didn't… Mike, can you and the kids show me the swing while we wait? I'm good at pushing.'

'Em asked you to order a cake?' Adrianna demanded, puzzled, and Oliver spread his hands.

'I crashed into her car this morning. She's been run off her legs all day and I asked if there was anything I could do. Therefore, in twenty minutes there'll be cake. Swing? Kids?'

'Oliver…' Em started, but Oliver put up his hand as if to stop her in mid-sentence. Which was exactly what he intended.

'She always wants to pay,' he told his ex-mother-in-law, grinning. 'She's stubborn as an ox, your Em, but you'd know that, Adrianna. We seem to have been arguing about money all day. I told you, Em, I'm doing the cake, you're on the balloons. Sorry I've mistimed it, though. I'll pay ten percent of the balloons to compensate. Any questions?'

'N-no,' Em said weakly, and his grin widened.

'How about that? No problems at all. Prepare for cake, Adrianna, and prepare for Birthday.'

And suddenly he was being towed outside by

kids who realised bedtime was being set back and birthday cake was in the offing. Leaving an open-mouthed Em and Adrianna in the kitchen.

Two minutes later, Mike was onside. They were pushing kids on swings and Oliver was on the phone. And it worked. His backup plan had been a fast trip to the supermarket for an off-the-shelf cake and blow-them-up-yourself balloons but, yes, the shop he remembered had decorated ice cream cakes. They were usually pre-ordered but if he was prepared to pay more... How fast could they pipe Adrianna's name on top? Candles included? Could they order a taxi to deliver it and charge his card? Did they do balloons? Next door did? Was it still open? How much to bung some of those in the taxi as well? He'd pay twice the price for their trouble.

'You're a fast mover,' Mike said, assessing him with a long, slow look as they pushed the double swing together. And then he said, not quite casually, 'Should I worry? If Em gets hurt I might just be tempted to do a damage.'

So Em had a protector. Good. Unless that protector was threatening to pick him up by the collar and hurl him off the property. He sighed and raked his hair and tried to figure how to respond.

'Mate, I'm not a fast mover,' he said at last. 'For five years I haven't moved at all. I'm not sure even what's happening here, but I'm sure as hell not moving fast.'

'Oh, Em, you remembered.' The moment the boys were out of the house Adrianna stooped and enveloped Em—and Gretta—in a bear hug. 'I've been thinking all day that no one's remembered and... Oh, sweetheart, I'm sorry.'

'You're sorry!' Em struggled to her feet, still cradling Gretta. She should confess, she thought, but as she looked at her mum's face she thought, no. Confession might make her feel better, but right now Adrianna was happy because her daughter had remembered. Oliver had given her that gift and she'd accept, because to do anything else would be cruel. Her mum did so much...

Oliver had rescued her. It'd be dumb to spoil his efforts with more than Adrianna had to know.

But she wasn't going to be dishonest. Not entirely. 'Mum, I remembered when I woke up this morning,' she said. 'But when Gretta was sick

I forgot to say it. It was such a rush all day and there's been nothing I could do. But when I met Oliver—'

'You knew he was coming?'

'He ordered the cake. And you know he's always loved you.' And that at least was the truth.

'Oh, Em...'

'And I've bought you a half-day spa voucher.' Yeah, she was lying about that but she could order and get it printed tonight. 'And if we can, I'll do it with you.' That's what Adrianna would like most in the world, she knew, but how would she manage that? But she looked at her mum's tired face and thought she had to do it. It might have to wait until Gretta was better, but she would do it.

If Gretta got better.

'Oh, but, Em...Gretta...'

'It can't be all about Gretta,' Em said gently, and that, too, was true. No matter how much attention Gretta needed, there were others who needed her, as well. It'd be a wrench to spend one of her precious free days...

But, no. This was her mum.

Oliver had saved the situation for now. The least she could do was take it forward.

* * *

The cake was amazing, an over-the-top confection that made the kids gasp with wonder. The taxi driver brought it in with a flourish then directed the kids to bring in the balloons. Whatever Oliver had paid, Em thought numbly, it must have been well and truly over the top, as the balloons were already filled, multi-coloured balls of floating air, bursting from the cab as soon as the doors were open, secured only by ribbons tied to the cab doors.

The kids brought them in, bunch upon bunch, and the kitchen was an instant party.

Katy arrived from next door, summoned by her kids. She wouldn't come right in—her flushed face verified her self-diagnosis of a streaming head cold and she declared there was no way she was risking Gretta catching anything—but she stood in the doorway and sang 'Happy Birthday' with the rest of them and watched while Adrianna blew out the candles and sliced the creamy caramel and chocolate and strawberry confection into slices that were almost cake-sized each.

'I can't believe it,' Adrianna said mistily, between mouthfuls of cake. 'Thank you all so much.'

And Em looked across at Oliver, who was sitting with Toby on his knee, one spoonful for Oliver, one spoonful for Toby, and she caught his gaze and tried to smile. But it didn't come off.

This was how it could have been, she thought. This was what she'd dreamed of.

But she'd pushed too hard, too fast. Josh's death had gutted her. She remembered sobbing, 'I can't do IVF any more, I'm too tired. There are babies out there who need us. We'll adopt. You're adopted, Oliver, you know it can work.'

But: 'It doesn't work,' he'd said, not angrily, just flatly, dully, stating immutable facts. 'It's second best and you know it.'

His reaction had shocked her. She'd been in no mood to compromise, and suddenly everything had escalated. The tension of five years of trying for a family had suddenly exploded. Leaving them with nothing.

What had he been doing for five years? Building his career, by the look of his CV. Turning into a wonderful doctor.

A caring doctor… His patience with two-year-old Toby, not the easiest kid to feed, was wonderful. The way he responded to the kids around the table, the mess, the laughter…

The way he smiled up at Adrianna and told her he was so sorry he'd missed her last five birthdays, she'd have to have five slices of cake to make up for it…

He was wonderful.

She wanted to weep.

She wanted to set Gretta down, walk around the table and hug him. Hold him.

Claim him again as her husband?

Right, like that was about to happen. The past was the past. They'd made their decisions and they'd moved on.

'Em's given me an afternoon at the day spa,' Adrianna said happily, cutting across her thoughts. Or almost. Her thoughts were pretty intense right now, pretty much centred on the gorgeous guy with the toddler, right across the table from her. She was watching his hands. She'd loved those hands—surgeon's hands. She remembered what those hands had been able to do.

She remembered…

'That's gorgeous,' Katy was saying from the doorway. 'But, Em, you still haven't had that colour and cut Mike and I gave you for Christmas. Right, Adrianna, this time it's going to work. As soon as I get over my snuffles I'm taking all five kids and you two are having your Christmas and birthday treats combined. This weekend?'

Once again, right. As if. Em gave her a smile, and then went to hug Adrianna, but she thought Katy would still be recovering by this weekend and her boys would probably catch her cold after her and Gretta was still so weak…

Adrianna should—and would—have her day spa but there'd be no day spas or colour and cuts for Em until…until…

The *until* was unthinkable. She hugged Gretta and her mind closed.

'What about this Saturday and using me?' Oliver asked, and she blinked. Had she misheard?

'You?'

'Anyone can see you've got the cold from hell,' he told Katy. 'Even if you're not still contagious you'll be wiped out, and you have three of your own to look after. Whereas I've just moved to Melbourne and my job hasn't geared up yet. There's nothing to stop me coming by and taking care of a couple of kids for a few hours.' He spooned chocolate ice-cream cake into Toby's waiting mouth and grinned at the little boy. 'Piece of cake, really. We'll have fun.' And then he smiled across at Gretta, focusing entirely on the little girl. 'How about it, Gretta? Will you let me take care of you and Toby?'

Gretta gazed back at him, clearly not understanding what was happening, but Oliver was smiling and she responded to the smile. She tried a tentative one of her own.

She was one brave kid, Oliver thought. But she looked so vulnerable... Her colour... Oxygen wasn't getting through.

'That'd be fantastic,' Adrianna breathed. 'Em worries about Gretta's breathing, but with you being a doctor...'

'Is he a doctor?' Katy demanded.

'He's Em's ex,' Mike growled, throwing a suspicious, hard stare at Oliver.

'But I'm still reliable,' Oliver said—hopefully—and Katy laughed.

'Hey, I hooked with some weirdos in my time,' she told the still-glowering Mike. 'But a couple of them turned into your mates. Just because they didn't come up to my high standards doesn't mean they're total failures as human beings. What do you say, Em? Trust your kids for a few hours with your ex? And him a doctor and all. It sounds an offer too good to refuse to me.'

And they were all looking at her. From what had started as a quiet night she was suddenly surrounded by birthday, kids, mess, chaos, and here was Oliver, threatening to walk into her life again.

No. Not threatening. Offering.

She'd been feeling like she was being bulldozed. Now... She looked at Oliver and he returned her gaze, calmly, placidly, like he was no threat at all. Whatever he'd been doing for the last five years it was nothing to do with her, but she knew one thing. He was a good man. She might not know him any more, but she could trust him, and if a specialist obstetrician and surgeon couldn't look after her Gretta, who could?

Her mind was racing. Gretta and Toby were both accustomed to strangers minding them—too many stays in hospital had seen to that. Oliver was currently feeding Toby like a pro.

She *could* take Adrianna for an afternoon out. She glanced again at her mum and saw the telltale flicker of hope in her eyes. She was so good... Without Adrianna, Em couldn't have these kids.

The fact that she'd once hoped to have them with Oliver...

No. Don't go there. She hauled herself back from the brink, from the emotions of five years ago, and she managed a smile at Oliver.

'Thank you, then,' she said simply. 'Thank you for offering. Mum and I would love it. Two p.m. on Saturday? We'll be back by five.'

'I'll be here at one.'

Four hours... Did she trust him that long?

Of course she did, she told herself. She did trust him. It was only... She needed to trust herself, as well. She needed to figure out the new way of the world, where Oliver Evans was no longer a lover or a husband.

It seemed Oliver Evans was offering to be a friend.

An hour later she was walking him out to his car. Amazingly, he'd helped put the kids to bed. 'If I'm to care for them on Saturday, they should see me as familiar.' The children had responded to his inherent gentleness, his teasing, his smile, and Em was struggling not to respond, as well.

But she was responding. Of course she was. How could she not? She'd fallen in love with this man a decade ago and the traces of that love remained. Life had battered them, pushed them apart, but it was impossible to think of him other than a friend.

Just a friend? He had to be. She'd made the decision five years ago—Oliver or children. She'd wanted children so much that she'd made her choice but it had been like chopping a part of herself out. Even now... The decision had been made in the aftermath of a stillbirth, when her emotions had been all over the place. If she was asked to make such a decision again...

She'd make it, she thought, thinking of the children in the house behind her. Gretta and Toby. Where would they be without her?

Someone else might have helped them, she thought, but now they were hers, and she loved them so fiercely it hurt.

If she'd stayed with Oliver she would have had... nothing.

'Tell me about the kids,' he said, politely almost,

leaning back on the driver's door of his car. His rental car.

It had been a lovely car she'd destroyed. That's what Oliver must have decided, she thought. He'd have a gorgeous car instead of kids—and now she'd smashed it.

'I'm sorry about your car,' she managed.

He made an exasperated gesture—leave it, not important. But it was important. She'd seen his face when he'd looked at the damage.

'Tell me about the kids,' he said again. 'You're fostering?'

'Mum and I decided…when you left…'

'To have kids?'

'You know I can't,' she said, evenly now, getting herself back together. 'For the year after you left I wasn't…very happy. I had my work as a midwife. I love my work, but you know that was never enough. And then one of my mums had Gretta.'

'One of your mums.'

'I know… Not very professional, is it, to get so personally involved? But Gretta was Miriam's third child. Miriam's a single mum who hadn't bothered to have any prenatal checks so missed the scans. From the moment the doctors told her

Gretta had Down's she hadn't wanted anything to do with her. Normally, Social Services can find adoptive parents for a newborn, even if it has Down's, but Miriam simply checked herself out of hospital and disappeared. We think she's in Western Australia with a new partner.'

'So you've taken her baby...'

'I didn't take her baby,' she said, thinking suddenly of the way he'd reacted to her suggestion of adoption all those years ago. It had been like adoption was a dirty word.

'I wasn't accusing...'

'No,' she said and stared down at her feet. She needed new shoes, she thought inconsequentially. She wore lace-up trainers—they were the most practical for the running she had to do—and a hole was starting to appear at her left big toe. Not this pay, she thought. Maybe next? Or maybe she could stick a plaster over the toe and pretend it was a new fashion. One of the kids' plasters with frogs on.

'What do you know about Miriam?' Oliver asked, and she hauled her attention back to him. Actually, it had never really strayed. But distractions were good. Distractions were necessary.

'We…we don't hear from Miriam,' she told him. 'But it's not for want of trying. Her two older children are in foster care together on a farm up near Kyneton—they're great kids and Harold and Eve are a wonderful foster-mum and dad—but Gretta couldn't go with them. Her heart problems have meant constant hospitalisation. We knew from the start that her life would be short. We knew it'd be a fight to keep her alive, so there was a choice. She could stay in hospital, institutionalised until she died, or I could take her home. She stayed in hospital for two months and then I couldn't bear it. Mum and I reorganised our lives and brought her home.'

'But she will die.' He said it gently, as if he was making sure she knew, and she flushed.

'You think we don't know that? But look at her tonight. She loved it. She loves…us.'

'I guess…'

'And don't you dare bring out your "Well, if she's adopted you can't possibly love her like your own" argument to say when she dies it won't hurt,' she snapped, suddenly unable to prevent the well of bitterness left from an appalling scene five years ago. 'We couldn't possibly love her more.'

'I never said that you couldn't love an adopted child.'

'Yes, you did.'

'I just said it's different and I hold by that. It's not the same love as from birth parents and you know it.'

'As Miriam's love? No, it's not and isn't Gretta lucky that it's not?'

'Em...'

'What?' She had her hands on her hips now, glaring. He'd shocked her so much, all those years ago. She'd been totally gutted when Josh had been stillborn, devastated beyond belief. She'd curled into a tight ball of misery, she'd hardly been able to function, but when finally daylight had begun to filter through the blackness, she'd clung to what had seemed her only hope.

'Oliver, let's stop with the in-vitro stuff. It's tearing me apart—it's tearing us apart. Let's try instead for adoption.'

But his reaction had stunned her.

'Em, no.' He'd said it gently but the words had been implacable. *'I can't guarantee to love a child who's not my own. I won't do that to a child.'*

It had been a divide neither of them could cross.

She had been so desperate for a child that she couldn't accept his refusal to consider adoption—and Oliver had walked away rather than concede.

'I love Gretta and so does Adrianna,' she said now, forcing herself to stay calm. Forcing herself to put the hurt of years ago on the back burner. 'So, moving on…'

'Toby?'

And mentioning her son's name was a sure way to defuse anger. Even saying his name made her smile.

'Adrianna found Toby,' she told him. 'Or rather Adrianna helped Toby find us.'

'Would you like to tell me about him?'

She'd prefer not to, actually. She was finding it disturbing on all sorts of levels to stand outside in the dusk with this man who'd once been her husband. But he had offered to take the children on Saturday, and she did need help. These last few months, with Gretta's health deteriorating, had been taking their toll on Adrianna. This Saturday would be gold for both of them, she knew, and Oliver had offered.

Therefore she had to be courteous. She had to share.

She had to stand outside with him a moment longer, even though a part of her wanted to turn around and run.

Why?

It was how he made her feel. It was the way her body was responding. He'd been her husband. She'd thought she knew this man at the deepest, most primeval level—yet here he was, standing in the dusk asking polite questions about children he knew nothing about.

Her children.

'Toby has multiple problems.' Somehow she'd pulled herself together…sort of. 'He's African, as you can probably guess. He has scoliosis of the spine; his spine was so bent he looked deformed even when he was born, and his family abandoned him. One of the poorest families in the village took him in. His pseudo-mum did the best she could for him but he hadn't been fed properly and he was already suffering from noma—a facial bacterial infection. She walked for three days to the nearest hospital to get him help—can you imagine that? But then, of course, she had to go back to her own family. But she'd fought for him first. One of the international aid agencies took on his case and brought him over here for facial reconstruction. So far he's been through six operations. He's doing great but...'

'But you can't keep him.'

She stilled. 'Why not? The hospital social worker in charge of his case knew Adrianna and I were already fostering Gretta, and she took a chance, asking us if we'd be willing to take him on. Adrianna did all the paperwork. Mum drove this, but we both want it. Theoretically he's supposed to go home when he's been treated. We're still in touch with his African foster-mum but she's so poor and she's very happy that he stays here. So in practice we're fighting tooth and nail to keep him.'

'Em, for heaven's sake...' He sounded appalled. 'You can't look after the world's waifs and strays. There are too many.'

'I can look after the ones I love,' she threw back at him, and tilted her chin. Defiant. She knew this argument—and here it came.

'You can't love him.'

'Why not?'

'He's not your kid.'

'Then whose kid is he? The woman who bore

him? The woman who walked for three days to save him but can't afford to feed him? Or Mum and me, who'll do our damnedest to keep him healthy and safe?'

'Em...' He raked his hair, a gesture she knew all too well. 'To take two kids like Gretta and Toby... A kid who'll die and a kid you might lose. They'll break your heart.'

'You just said I can't love them. You can't have it both ways, Oliver.'

'Is this what you wanted me to do? Adopt the kids the world's abandoned?'

'I don't think I expected anything of you,' she managed, and was inordinately proud of how calm she sounded. 'At the end of our marriage all I could see was what I needed. I know that sounds selfish, and maybe it is, but it's what I desperately wanted. Despite loving you I couldn't stop that wanting. You always knew I wanted a family. I'm a midwife, and I'm a midwife because watching babies come into the world is what I love most. I'd dreamed we could have our own family...'

'And when that didn't happen you walked away.'

'As I remember it, you walked.'

'Because it's not fair for me to adopt. These kids need their own parents.'

'They don't have them. Are you saying second best is worse than nothing?'

'They'll know…that they're second best.'

'Oliver, just because that happened to you…'

And she watched his face close, just like that.

He didn't talk about it, she thought. He'd never talked about it but she'd guessed.

She thought, fleetingly, of her in-laws, of Oliver's adoptive parents. But she had to think fleetingly because thinking any more made her so angry she could spit.

She only knew the bare bones but it was enough. She could infer the rest. They'd had trouble conceiving so they'd adopted Oliver. Then, five years later, they'd conceived naturally and their own son had been born.

Oliver never talked about it—never would talk about it—but she'd seen the family in action. Brett was five years younger than Oliver, a spoiled brat when Em had first met him and now an obnoxious, conceited young man who thought the world owed him a living.

But his parents thought the sun shone from him,

and it seemed to Em that they'd spent their lives comparing their two sons, finding fault with Oliver and setting Brett on a pedestal.

Even at their wedding...

'He's done very well for himself,' Em had over-heard his adoptive mother tell an aunt. *'Considering where he comes from. We've done what we could, but still... I know he's managed to get himself qualified as a doctor but... His mother was a whore, you know, and we can never forget that. Thank God we have Brett.'*

It had been as much as Em could do not to front the woman and slap her. It wouldn't have been a good look on her wedding day—bride smacks mother-in-law—but she'd come awfully close. But Oliver had never talked of it.

It was only when the adoption thing had come up when Josh had died that the ghosts had come from nowhere. And she couldn't fight them, for Oliver wouldn't speak of them.

'Oliver, we're doing our best,' she told him now, gentling, reminding herself that it was his ghosts talking, not him. She knew it was his ghosts, but she'd never been allowed close enough to fight them. 'Mum and I are loving these kids to bits. We're doing all we possibly can...'

'It won't be enough.'

'Maybe it won't.' She was suddenly bone weary again. Understanding could only go so far. 'But we're trying the best that we can. We'll give these kids our hearts, and if that's not enough to let them thrive then we'll be incredibly sad but we won't be regretful. We have love to give and we're giving it. We're trying, whereas you... You lacked courage to even think about it. "No adoptions," you said, end of story. I know your background. I know how hard it was for you to be raised with Brett but your parents were dumb and cruel. The whole world doesn't have to be like that.'

'And if you ever had a child of your own?'

'You're saying I shouldn't go near Gretta or Toby because I might, conceivably, still have a child biologically?'

'I didn't mean that.' He raked his hair again, in that gesture she'd known and loved. She had a sudden urge to rake it herself, settle it, touch his face, take away the pain.

Because there was pain. She could see it. This man was torn.

But she couldn't help him if he wouldn't talk about it. To be helped you had to admit you needed help. He'd simply closed off, shut her out, and there was nothing she could do about it.

She'd moved on, but he was still hurting. She couldn't help him.

'Go home,' she said, gently again. 'I'm sorry, Oliver, I have no right to bring up the past, but neither do you have a right to question what I'm doing. Our marriage is over and we need to remember it. We need to finalise our divorce. Meanwhile, thank you for tonight, for Adrianna's birthday. I'm deeply appreciative, but if you want to pull out of Saturday's childminding, I understand.'

'I'll be here.'

'You don't need to...'

'I will be here.'

'Fine, then,' she said, and took a step back in the face of his sudden blaze of anger. 'That's good. That's great. I'll see you then.'

'I'll see you at the hospital tomorrow,' he said. 'With Ruby.'

And her heart sank. Of course. She was going to see this man, often. She needed to work with him.

She needed to ignore the pain she still saw in his eyes. She needed to tell herself, over and over, that it had nothing to do with her.

The problem was, that wasn't Em's skill. Ignoring pain.

But he didn't want her interference. He never had.

He didn't want her.

Moving on…

'Goodnight, then,' she managed, and she couldn't help herself. She touched his face with her hand and then stood on tiptoe and lightly kissed him—a feather touch, the faintest brush of lips against lips. 'Goodnight, Oliver. I'm sorry for your demons but your demons aren't mine. I give my heart for always, non-negotiable, adoption, fostering, marriage… Ollie, I can no more change myself than fly. I'm just sorry you can't share.'

And she couldn't say another word. She was suddenly so close to tears that she pushed away and would have stumbled.

Oliver's hand came out to catch her. She steadied and then brushed him off. She did it more roughly than she'd intended but she was out of her depth.

'Thank you,' she whispered, and turned away. 'Goodnight.' And she turned and fled into the house.

Oliver was left standing in the shadows, watching the lights inside the house, knowing he should leave, knowing he had to.

'I give my heart for always.'

What sort of statement was that?

She'd been talking about the kids, he told himself, but still...

She'd included marriage in the statement, and it was a statement to give a man pause.

CHAPTER SIX

EM HARDLY SAW Oliver the next day. The maternity ward was busy, and when she wasn't wanted in the birthing suites, she mostly stayed with Ruby.

The kid was so alone. Today was full of fill-in-the-blanks medical forms and last-minute checks, ready for surgery the next day. The ultrasounds, the visit and check by the anaesthetist, the constant checking and rechecking that the baby hadn't moved, that the scans that had shown the problem a week ago were correct, that they had little choice but to operate… Everything was necessary but by the end of the day Ruby was ready to get up and run.

She needed her mum, a sister, a mate, anyone, Em thought. That she was so alone was frightening. Isla dropped in for a while. Ruby was part of Isla's teen mums programme and Ruby relaxed with her, but she was Ruby's only visitor.

'Isn't there anyone I can call?' Em asked as the day wore on and Ruby grew more and more tense.

'No one'll come near me,' Ruby said tersely. 'Mum said if I didn't have an abortion she'd wash her hands of me. She said if I stayed near her I'd expect her to keep the kid and she wasn't having a thing to do with it. And she told my sisters they could stay away, too.'

'And your baby's father?'

'I told you before, the minute I told him about it, he was off. Couldn't see him for dust.'

'Oh, Ruby, there must be someone.'

'I'll be okay,' Ruby said with bravado that was patently false. 'I'll get this kid adopted and then I'll get a job in a shop or something. I just wish it was over now.'

'We all wish that.'

And it was Oliver again. He moved around the wards like a great prowling cat, Em thought crossly. He should wear a bell.

'What?' he demanded, as she turned towards him, and she thought she really had to learn to stop showing her feelings on her face.

'Knock!'

'Sorry. If I'm intruding I'll go away.'

'You might as well come in and poke me, too,' Ruby sighed. 'Everyone else has. I'm still here. Bub's still here. Why is everyone acting like we're about to go up in smoke before tomorrow? Why do I need to stay in bed?'

'Because we need your baby to stay exactly where she is,' Oliver told her, coming further into the room. He had a bag under his arm and Ruby eyed it with suspicion. 'Right now she's in the perfect position to operate on her spine, and, no, Ruby, there's not a single thing in this bag that will prod, poke or pry. But I would like to feel your baby for myself.'

Ruby sighed with a theatrical flourish and tugged up her nightie.

'Go ahead. Half the world already has.'

'Has she moved?'

'Nah.' She gave a sheepish grin. 'I feel her myself. I'm not stupid, you know.' And she popped her hand on her tummy and cradled it.

There was that gesture again. Protective. *'Mine.'*

Oliver sat down on the bed and felt the rounded bump himself, and Em looked at the way he was examining the baby and thought this was a skill. Ruby had been poked and prodded until she was tired of it. Oliver was doing the same thing but very gently, as if he was cradling Ruby's unborn child.

'She's perfect,' he said at last, tugging Ruby's nightie back down. 'Like her mother.'

'She's not perfect. That's why I'm here.'

'She's pretty much perfect. Would you like to see a slide show of what we're about to do?' He grinned at Ruby's scared expression. 'There's not many gory bits and I can fast-forward through them.'

'I'll shut my eyes,' Ruby said, but he'd caught her, Em thought. She wasn't dissociated from this baby. Once again she saw Ruby's hand move surreptitiously to her tummy.

He flicked open his laptop. Fascinated, Em perched on the far side of the bed and watched, too.

'This is one we prepared earlier,' Oliver said, in the tone TV cooks used as they pulled a perfect bake from the oven. 'This is Rufus. He's six months old now, a lovely, healthy baby, but at the start of this he was still inside his mum, a twenty-two-weeker. This is the procedure your little one will have.'

The screen opened to an operating theatre, the patient's face hidden, the film obviously taken for teaching purposes as identities weren't shown. But the sound was on, and Em could hear Oliver's voice, calmly directive, and she knew that it was Oliver who was in charge.

She was fascinated—and so was Ruby. Squeamishness was forgotten. They watched in awe as the scalpel carefully, carefully negotiated the layers between the outside world and the baby within. It would be an intricate balance, Em knew, trying to give the baby minimal exposure to the outside world, keeping infection out, disturbing the baby as little as possible yet giving the surgeons space to work.

There were many doctors present—she could hear their voices. This was cutting-edge surgery.

'I can see its back,' Ruby breathed. 'Oh…is that the same as my baby?'

'They're all different,' Oliver said. 'Your daughter is tilted at a better angle.'

'Oh…' Ruby's eyes weren't leaving the screen.

They could definitely see the baby now, and they could see how the baby was slightly tilted to the side. Carefully, carefully Oliver manoeuvred him within the uterus, making no sudden movements, making sure the move was no more dramatic than if the baby himself had wriggled.

And now they could see the spine exposed. The telltale bulge…

'Is that the problem? The same as mine?' Ruby whispered, and Oliver nodded.

'Rufus's problem was slightly lower, but it's very similar.'

Silence again. They were totally focused, all of them. Oliver must have seen this many times before, Em thought—and he'd been there in person—but he was still watching it as if it was a miracle.

It was a miracle.

'This is where I step back and let the neurosurgeon take over,' Oliver said. 'My job is to take care of the whole package, you and your baby, but Dr Zigler will be doing this bit. He's the best, Ruby. You're in the best of hands.'

They watched on. The surgery was painstaking. It was like microsurgery, Em thought, where fingers were reattached, where surgeons fought hard to save nerves. And in a way it was. They were carefully working around and then through the bulge. There'd be so many things to work around. The spinal cord was so fragile, so tiny. The task was to repair the damage already done, as far as possible, and then close, protecting the cord and peripheral nerves from the amniotic fluid until the baby was born.

'Is…is it hurting?' Ruby breathed, as the first incision was made into the tiny back.

'Is *he* hurting? No. Rufus is anaesthetised, as well as his mum. Did you see the anaesthetist working as soon as we had exposure? The jury's out on whether unborn babies can feel pain. There are those who say they're in a state similar to an induced coma, but they certainly react to a painful touch. It makes the procedure a little more risky—balancing anaesthetic with what he's receiving via his mum's blood supply—but the last thing we want is to stress him. Luckily the Victoria has some of the best anaesthetists in the world. Vera Harty will be doing your anaesthetic and your daughter's. I'd trust her with a baby of my own.'

Ruby was satisfied. She went back to watching the screen.

Em watched, too, but Oliver's last statement kept reverberating.

I'd trust her with a baby of my own.

The sadness was flooding back. Oliver had been unable to have a baby of his own—because of her. She had fertility problems, not Oliver.

He'd left her years ago. He could have found someone by now.

Maybe he had. Maybe he just wasn't saying.

But he hadn't. She knew him well, this man.

There'd been an undercurrent of longing in the statement.

They'd both wanted children. She'd released him so he could have them. Why hadn't he moved on?

Watch the screen, she told herself. Some things were none of her business. Oliver was none of her business—except he was the obstetrician treating her patient.

She went back to being professional—sort of. She went back to watching Rufus, as Oliver and Ruby were doing.

The procedure was delicate and it took time but it seemed Oliver was in no hurry to finish watching, and neither was Ruby. Em couldn't be, either. Her job was to keep Ruby calm for tomorrow's operation, and that's what was happening now. The more familiar the girl was about what lay ahead, the more relaxed she'd be.

And not for the first time, Em blessed this place, this job. The Victoria considered its mid-wives some of the most important members of its staff. The mothers' needs came first and if a mum needed her midwife then Isla would some-how juggle the rest of her staff to cover.

Unless there was major drama Em wouldn't be interrupted now, she thought, and she wasn't. They made an intimate trio, midwife and doc-tor, with Ruby sandwiched between. Protected? That's what it felt like to Em, and she suspected that's how Ruby felt. Had Oliver set this up with just this goal? She glanced at him and knew her suspicion was right.

The first time she'd met him she'd been awed by his medical skills. Right now, watching him operate on screen, feeling Ruby's trust growing by the second, that awe was escalating into the stratosphere.

He might not make it as a husband, but he surely made it as a surgeon.

Back on screen, the neurosurgeon was suturing,

using careful, painstakingly applied, tiny stitches, while Oliver was carefully monitoring the levels of amniotic fluid. This baby would be born already scarred, Em thought. He'd have a scar running down his lower back—but with luck that was all he'd have. Please...

'It worked a treat,' Oliver said, sounding as pleased as if the operation had happened yesterday, and on screen the neurosurgeon stood back and Oliver took over. The final stitches went in, closing the mum's uterus, making the incision across the mum's tummy as neat as the baby's. 'Rufus was born by Caesarean section at thirty-three weeks,' Oliver told them. 'He spent four weeks in hospital as a prem baby but would you like to see him now?'

'I... Yes.' Ruby sounded as if she could scarcely breathe.

'We have his parents' permission to show him to other parents facing the same procedure,' Oliver told her. 'Here goes.'

He fiddled with the computer and suddenly they were transported to a suburban backyard, to a rug thrown on a lawn, to a baby, about six months old, lying on his back in the sun, kicking his legs, admiring his toes.

There was a dog at the edge of the frame, a dopey-looking cocker spaniel. As they watched, the dog edged forward and licked the baby's toes. Rufus crowed with laughter and his toes went wild.

'He doesn't…he doesn't look like there's anything wrong with him,' Ruby breathed.

'He still has some issues he needs help with.' Oliver was matter-of-fact now, surgeon telling it like it was. 'He'll need physiotherapy to help him walk, and he might need professional help to learn how to control his bladder and bowels, but the early signs are that he'll be able to lead a perfectly normal life.'

'He looks…perfect already.' Ruby was riveted and so was Em. She was watching Ruby's face. She was watching Ruby's hand, cradling her bump. 'My little one…my little girl…she could be perfect, too?'

'I think she already is.' Oliver was smiling down at her. 'She has a great mum who's taking the best care of her. And you have the best midwife…'

Em flashed him a look of surprise. There was no need to make this personal.

But for Ruby, this was nothing but personal. 'Em says she'll stay with me,' Ruby told him. 'At the operation and again when my baby's born. There's a chance that she can't—she says no one's ever totally sure because babies are unpredictable—but she's promised to try. I hope she can, but if she's not then she's introduced me to Sophia, or Isla will take over. But you'll look after...' Her hand cradled the bump again as she looked anxiously at Oliver. 'You'll look after us both?'

'I will.' And it was a vow.

'Tell me again why I need a Caesarean later—when my baby's born properly?'

He nodded, closed his laptop and sat back in a visitor's chair, to all appearances prepared to chat for as long as Ruby wanted. He was busy, Em knew. As well as the promises he'd made her to childmind on Saturday, she knew he already had a full caseload of patients. But right now Ruby was being given the impression that he had all the time in the world, and that time was Ruby's.

He was...gorgeous. She knew it, she'd always

known it, but suddenly the thought almost blind-sided her.

And it was more than him being gorgeous, she thought, feeling dazed. She was remembering why she'd loved this man.

And she was thinking—idiotically—that she loved him still.

Concentrate on medicine, on your patient, on anything other than Oliver, she told herself fiercely. Concentrating on Oliver was just too scary.

What had Ruby asked? Why she needed a Cae-sarean?

'You see the incision we just cut in Rufus's mum's uterus?' Oliver was saying, flicking back to the screen, where they could see the now closed incision in the abdomen. 'I've stitched it with care, as I'll stitch you with care, but when your bub comes out, she'll push. You have no idea how hard a baby can push. She wants to get out to meet you, and nothing's going to stop her. So maybe she'll push against that scar, and if she pushes hard enough on very new scar tissue she might cause you to bleed. I have two people I care about, Ruby. I care about your daughter but my absolute priority is to keep you safe. That means a Caesarean birth, because, much as I want to meet your baby, we'll need to deliver her before she even thinks about pushing.'

'But if you wanted to keep me really safe you wouldn't operate in the first place,' Ruby muttered, a trace of the old resentment resurfacing. But it didn't mess with Oliver's composure.

'That's right,' he agreed, his tone not changing. 'I believe we *will* keep you safe but there are risks. They're minor but they're real. That's why it's your choice. You can still pull out. Right up to the time we give you the anaesthetic, you can pull out, and no one will think the worse of you. That's your right.'

The room fell silent. It was such a hard decision to make, Em thought, and once again she thought, Where was this kid's mum?

But, surprisingly, when Ruby spoke again it seemed that worry about the operation was being supplanted by something deeper.

'If I had her...' Ruby said, and then amended her statement. '*When* I have her...after she's born, she'll have a scar, too.'

'She will,' Oliver told her, as watchful as Em, waiting to know where Ruby was going with this.

'And she'll have it for ever?

'Yes.'

'She might hate it—as a teenager,' Ruby whispered. 'I know I would.'

'I'll do my best to make it as inconspicuous as possible—and cosmetic touch-ups when she's older might help even more. It shouldn't be obvious.'

'But teenagers freak out about stuff like that. I know I would,' Ruby whispered. 'And she won't have a mum to tell her it's okay.'

'If she's adopted, she'll have a mum,' Em ventured. 'Ruby, we've gone through what happens. Adoption is your choice all the way. You'll get to meet the adoptive parents. You'll know she goes to parents who'll love her.'

'But...I'll love her more. She's *my* baby.'

And suddenly Ruby was crying, great fat tears slipping down her face, and Em shifted so she could take her into her arms. And as she did so, Oliver's laptop slid off the bed and landed with a crash on the floor.

Uh-oh. But Em didn't move. For now she

couldn't afford to think of computers. For now holding this girl was the most important thing in the world.

But still… A car and then a laptop…

She was starting to be an expensive ex-wife, she thought ruefully, and she almost smiled—but, of course, she didn't. She simply held Ruby until the sobs receded, until Ruby tugged away and grabbed a handful of tissues. That was a bit late. Em's shoulder was soaked, but who cared? How many times had Em ever finished a shift clean? She could count them on one hand. She always got her hands dirty, one way or another.

And it seemed, so did Oliver, for he was still there. Most consultants would have fled at the first sign of tears, Em thought. As a breed, surgeons weren't known for their empathy.

He'd risen, but he was standing by the door, watching, and there was definitely sympathy. Definitely caring.

He was holding the two halves of his laptop. The screen had completely split from the keyboard. And the screen itself…smashed.

'Whoops,' she said, as Ruby blew her nose.

He glanced down at the ruined machine. 'As you say, whoops.'

And as Ruby realised what he was holding, the teenager choked on something that was almost a laugh. 'Em's smashed your computer,' she said, awed. 'Do you mind?'

'I can't afford to mind.'

'Why not?' She was caught, pulled out of her misery by a smashed computer.

'Priorities,' he said. 'You. Baby. Computer. In that order.'

'What about Em?' she asked, a touch of cheekiness emerging. 'Is she a priority?'

'Don't you dare answer,' Em told him. 'Not until you've checked that your computer is covered by insurance. Ruby, if you're rethinking your plans to adopt...'

'I think...I might be.'

'Then let's not make any decisions yet,' she said, hurriedly. Surely now wasn't the time to make such an emotional decision? 'Let's get this operation over with first.'

Ruby took a deep breath and looked from Oliver to Emily and back again. 'Maybe I do need a bit of time,' she conceded. 'Maybe a sleep... time to think.'

'Of course you do.' She pulled up her covers and tucked her in. 'Ruby, nothing's urgent. No decisions need to be made now. Just sleep.'

'Thank you. And, Dr Evans...'

'Mmm?' Oliver was about to leave but turned back.

'I hope your computer's all right.'

'It will be,' he said. But it wouldn't. Em could see the smashed screen from where she stood. 'But even if it's not, it's not your problem,' he said, gently now, almost as a blessing. 'From here on, Ruby, we don't want you to worry about a thing. You've put yourself in our hands and we'll keep you safe. Em and I are a great team. You and your baby are safe with us.'

His lovely, gentle bedside manner lasted until they were ten feet from Ruby's door. Em closed the door behind her, looked ahead—and Oliver was staring straight at her. Vibrating with anger.

'You're planning on talking her out of keeping her baby?'

The turnabout from empathy to anger was

shocking. The gentleness had completely gone from his voice. What she saw now was fury.

She faced him directly, puzzled. 'What are you saying? I didn't. I'm not.'

'You are. She'd decided on adoption but now she's changing her mind. But you stopped her.'

'I didn't stop her. I'd never do that.' She thought back to the scene she'd just left, trying to replay her words. 'I just said she had time...'

'You told her not to make a decision now. Why not? Right now she's thinking of keeping her baby. You don't think it's important to encourage her?'

'I don't think it's my right to direct her one way or another.' She felt herself getting angry in response. 'All I saw in there was a frightened, tired kid who's facing major surgery tomorrow. Who needs to stay calm and focused. Who doesn't need to be making life-changing decisions right now. She's already decided enough.'

'But maybe when you're emotional, that's the time to make the decision. When she knows she loves her baby.'

'She'll always love her baby.' Em was struggling to stay calm in the face of his anger—in the face of his accusation? 'Ruby is a seventeen-year-old, terrified kid with no family support at all. If she decides to keep this baby, it'll change her life for ever. As it will if she gives it up for adoption. What I did in there—and, yes, I interceded—was give her space. If she wants to keep her baby, she'll need every ounce of strength and then some.'

'She'll get support.'

'And she can never be a kid again. But, then, after this, maybe being a kid is no longer an option. But I agree, that's none of my business. Oliver, is this discussion going anywhere? I've been away from the birthing suites for over an hour and I don't know what's going on. I may well be needed.'

'You won't influence her?'

'Why would I influence her?'

'Because you believe in adoption.'

'And you don't? Because of what happened to you when you were a kid?' Anger was washing over her now. Yes, she should get back to the birthing suites but what was it he was accusing her of? 'Get over it, Oliver. Move on. Not every adoptive mother is like yours, and not every birth mother is capable of loving. There's a whole lot of grey in between the black and white, and it's about time you saw it.'

'So you won't encourage her to adopt?'

'What are you expecting me to do?' She was confused now, as well as angry. She put her hands on her hips and glared. 'Are you thinking I might pop in there, offer to adopt it myself and get myself another baby? Is that what you're thinking?'

'I would never—'

'You'd better not. A midwife influencing a mother's decision is totally unethical. How much more so is a midwife offering to adopt? I'll do neither. I have my kids, Oliver, and I love them to bits. I have no wish for more.'

'But Gretta's going to die.'

Why had he said it? It had just come out, and he could have bitten his tongue from his head. Em's face bleached white and she leaned back against the wall for support.

Dear heaven… What sort of emotional drop kick was he? Suggesting one kid was going to die so she was lining up for another? Where had the thought come from?

It was confusion, he thought. Maybe it was even anger that she'd got on with her life without him.

Or maybe it was sheer power of testosterone washing through him—because the woman who should be his wife was looking at him as if he was a piece of dirt.

Where to start with apologies? He'd better haul himself back under control, and fast. 'Hell, Em, I'm sorry. I didn't mean that the way it came out, truly.' He reached out and touched her stricken face, and the way he felt...sick didn't begin to describe it. 'Can you forget I said it? Of all the insensitive oafs... I know Gretta's health has nothing to do with...anything. I'm so sorry. Can you wipe it? I know you love Gretta...'

'Are you talking about Emily's little girl?'

They both turned to face the newcomer, and it was a relief to turn away from each other. The tension between them was so tight it was threatening to break, to fly back and hit both of them.

Oliver recognised the young man heading towards them. Oliver had been introduced to Noah Jackson earlier in the week. He was a surgical registrar, almost at the end of his training. 'Technically brilliant,' Tristan, the paediatric cardiologist, had told him. 'But his people skills leave a whole lot to be desired.'

And now he proceeded to display just that.

'Hi, Em,' he called, walking up to them with breezy insouciance. 'Are you discussing Gretta's progress? How's she going?'

'She's…okay,' Em said, and by the way she said it Oliver knew there was baggage behind the question.

'You ought to meet Gretta,' Noah told Oliver, seemingly oblivious to the way Em's face had shuttered. 'She's worth a look. She has Down's, with atrioventricular septal defects, massive heart problems, so much deformity that even Tristan felt he couldn't treat her. Yet she's survived. I've collated her case notes from birth as part of my final-year research work. I'd love to write her up for the med journals. It'd give me a great publication. Em's care has been nothing short of heroic.'

'I've met her,' Oliver said shortly, glancing again at Em. Gretta—a research project? He could see Em's distress. 'Now's not…' he started.

But the young almost-surgeon wouldn't be stopped. 'Gretta wasn't expected to live for more than a year,' he said, with enthusiasm that wouldn't be interrupted. 'It'll make a brilliant article—the extent of the damage, the moral dilemma facing

her birth mother, her decision to walk away—
Em's decision to intervene and now the medical
resources and the effort to keep her alive this far.
Em, please agree to publication. You still haven't
signed. But Tristan says she's pretty close to the
end. If I could examine her one last time...'

And Oliver saw the wash of anger and revulsion
on Em's face—and finally he moved.

He put his body between the registrar and Em.
Noah was tall but right now Oliver felt a good
foot taller. Anger did that. Of all the insensitive...

'You come near Em again with your requests for
information about her daughter—her *daughter*,
Noah, not her patient—and I'll ram every page of
your case notes down your throat. Don't you realise that Em loves Gretta? Don't you realize she's
breaking in two, and you're treating her daughter
like a bug under a microscope?'

'Hey, Em's a medical colleague,' Noah said, still
not getting it. 'She knows the score—she knew it
when she took Gretta home. She can be professional.'

'Is that what you're being—professional?'

'If we can learn anything from this, then, yes...'

Enough. Em looked close to fainting.

The lift was open behind them. Oliver grabbed Noah by the collar of his white jacket, twisted him round and practically kicked him into the lift.

'What…?' Noah seemed speechless. 'What did I say?'

'You might be nearing the end of your surgical training,' Oliver snapped. 'But you sure aren't at the end of your training to be a decent doctor. You need to learn some people skills, fast. I assume you did a term in family medicine during your general training, but whether you did or not, you're about to do another. And another after that if you still don't get it. I want you hands-on, treating people at the coal face, before you're ever in charge of patients in a surgical setting.'

'You don't have that authority.' The young doctor even had the temerity to sound smug.

'You can believe that,' Oliver growled. 'You're welcome—for all the good it'll do you. Now get out of here while I see if I can fix the mess you've made.'

'I haven't made a mess.'

'Oh, yes, you have,' Oliver snapped, hitting the 'Close' button on the lift with as much force as he'd like to use on Noah. 'And you've messed with someone who spends her life trying to fix messes. Get out of my sight.'

The lift closed. Oliver turned back to Em. She hadn't moved. She was still slumped on the wall, her face devoid of colour. A couple of tears were tracking down her face.

'It's okay,' she managed. 'Oliver, it's okay. He's just saying it like it is.'

'He has no right to say anything at all,' Oliver snapped, and he couldn't help himself. She was so bereft. She was so gutted.

She was…his wife?

She wasn't. Their long separation to all intents and purposes constituted a divorce, but right now that was irrelevant.

His Em was in trouble. *His Em.*

He walked forward and took her into his arms.

She shouldn't let him hold her. She had no right to be in his arms.

She had no right to want to be in his arms.

Besides, his words had upset her as much as Noah's had. His implication that she could replace Gretta…

But she knew this man. She'd figured it out—

the hurt he'd gone through as a kid, the rejection, the knowledge that he'd been replaced by his adoptive parents' 'real' son.

Noah was just plain insensitive. He was arrogant and intelligent but he was lacking emotional depth. Oliver's comments came from a deep, long-ago hurt that had never been resolved.

And even if it hadn't, she thought helplessly, even if he was as insensitive as Noah, even if she shouldn't have anything to do with him, for now she wanted to be here.

To be held. By her husband.

For he still felt like her husband. They'd been married for five years. They'd lain in each other's arms for five years.

For five years she'd thought she had the perfect marriage.

But she hadn't. Of course she hadn't. There had been ghosts she'd been unable to expunge, and those ghosts were with him still. He couldn't see…

Stop thinking, she told herself fiercely, almost desperately. Stop thinking and just be. Just let his arms hold me. Just feel his heart beat against mine. Just pretend…

'Em, I'm sorry,' he whispered into her hair.

'For?'

'For what I said. Even before Noah, you were hurt. I can't begin to think how I could have said such a thing.'

'It doesn't matter.' But it did. It was the crux of what had driven them apart. For Oliver, adoption was simply a transaction. Hearts couldn't be held...

As theirs hadn't. Their marriage was over.

But still she held. Still she took comfort, where she had no right to take comfort. They'd been separated for five years!

So why did he still feel like...home? Why did everything about him feel as if here was her place in the world?

'Hey!' A hospital corridor was hardly the place to hold one's ex-husband—to hold anyone. It was busy and bustling and their sliver of intimacy couldn't last.

It was Isla, hurrying along the corridor, smiling—as Isla mostly smiled right now. The sapphire on her finger seemed to have changed Em's boss's personality. 'You know I'm all for romance,' she said as she approached. 'But the corridor's not the place.' She glanced down at the sapphire on her finger and her smile widened. 'Alessi and I find the tea room's useful. No one's in there right now...'

'Oh, Isla...' Em broke away, flushing. 'Sorry. It's not... Dr Evans was just...just...'

But Isla had reached them now and was seeing Em's distress for herself. 'Nothing's wrong with Ruby, is there?' she asked sharply.

'No.' Oliver didn't break his composure. 'But you have a problem with Dr Noah Jackson. He seems to think Em's Gretta is a research experiment.'

'Noah's been upsetting my midwife?' Isla's concern switched to anger, just like that. 'Let me at him.'

'I don't think there's any need,' Em managed. 'Oliver practically threw him into the lift.'

'Well, good for you,' Isla said, smiling again. 'I do like an obstetrician who knows when to act, and one who knows the value of a good cuddle is worth his weight in gold.' She glanced again at her ring. 'I should know. But, Em, love, if you've finished being cuddled, I would like you back in the birthing suite.'

'Of course,' Em said, and fled.

There was a moment's silence. Then…

'Don't you mess with my midwives,' Isla said, and Oliver looked at her and thought she saw a whole lot more than she let on.

'I won't.'

She eyed him some more. 'You two have baggage? Your name's the same.'

'We don't have…baggage.'

'I don't believe it.' She was still thoughtful. 'But I'll let it lie. All I'll say is to repeat—don't mess with my midwives.'

Thursday night was blessedly uneventful. Gretta seemed to have settled. Em should have had a good night's sleep.

She didn't but the fact that she stared into the dark and thought of Oliver was no fault of…anyone.

Oliver was no business of hers.

But he'd held her and he felt all her business.

Oliver…

Why had he come here to work? Of all the unlucky coincidences…

But it wasn't a simple coincidence, she conceded. The Victoria had one of Australia's busiest birthing units. It was also right near her mother's home so it had made sense that she get a job here after the loss of Josh.

And after the loss of Oliver.

Don't go there, she told herself. Think of practicalities.

It made sense that Oliver was back here, she told herself. Charles Delamere head-hunted the best, and he'd have known Oliver had links to Melbourne.

So she should leave?

Leave the Victoria? Because Oliver had…cuddled her?

It's not going to happen again, she told herself fiercely. And I won't leave because of him. There's no need to leave.

He could be a friend. Like Isla. Like Sophia.

Yeah, right, she told herself, punching her pillow in frustration. Oliver Evans, just a friend?

Not in a million years.

But she had no choice. She could do this. Bring on tomorrow, she told herself.

Bring on a way she could treat Oliver as a medical colleague and nothing else.

CHAPTER SEVEN

FRIDAY. EM'S DAY was cleared so she could focus on Ruby. Isla was aware of the situation. 'If she really has no one, then you'd better be with her all the way.'

So she stayed with Ruby in the hour before she was taken to Theatre. She spent their time discussing—of all things—Ruby's passion for sewing. Ruby had shyly shown her her handiwork the day before, so Em had brought in one of Toby's sweaters. Ruby was showing her how to darn a hole in the elbow.

'Darning's a dying art,' she'd told Em, so Em had found the sweater and brought a darning mushroom—Adrianna had one her grandmother had used!—and needle and thread and asked for help.

Ruby took exquisite care with the intricate patch. When she was finished Em could scarcely see where the hole had been, and darning and the concentration involved worked a charm. When the orderlies came to take Ruby to Theatre, Ruby was shocked that the time had already arrived.

She squeezed Em's hand. 'Th-thank you. Will I see you later?'

'I'm coming with you,' Em declared, packing up the darning equipment. 'Isla's told me if I'm to help deliver your baby at term then I should introduce myself to her now. So I'm to stay in the background, not faint, and admire Dr Evans's handiwork.'

'You'd never faint.'

'Don't you believe it,' Em told her, and proceeded to give her some fairly gross examples. She kept right up with the narrative while Ruby was pushed through to Theatre, while pre-meds were given, while they waited for the theatre to be readied. Finally, as Ruby was wheeled into Theatre, they were both giggling.

Oliver was waiting, gowned and ready. So, it seemed, was a cast of thousands. This was surgery at its most cutting edge. They were operating on two patients, not one, but one of those patients was a foetus that was not yet viable outside her mother. The logistics were mind-bending and it would take the combined skills of the Victoria's finest to see it succeed.

Shock to the foetus could cause abortion. Therefore the anaesthetic had to be just right—they had not only the Victoria's top anaesthetist, but also the anaesthetic registrar. Heinz Zigler was gowned and ready. Tristan Hamilton, paediatric cardiologist, was there to check on the baby's heart every step of the way. There were so many possible complications.

The surgery itself was demanding but everything else had to be perfect, as well. If amniotic fluid was lost it had to be replaced. If the baby bled, that blood had to be replaced, swiftly but so smoothly the loss couldn't be noticed. Everything had to be done with an eye to keeping the trauma to the baby at the absolute minimum.

'Hey, Ruby.' Oliver welcomed the girl warmly as she was wheeled in, and if he was tense he certainly wasn't showing it. 'What's funny?'

'Em's been telling me—' Ruby was almost asleep from the pre-meds but she was still smiling '—about muddles. About her work.'

'Did she tell you about the time she helped deliver twins and the team messed up their bracelets?' Oliver was smiling with his patient, but he found a chance to glance—and smile—at Em. 'So Mathew Riley was wrapped in a pink rug and Amanda Riley was wrapped in a blue rug. It could have scarred them for life.'

Em thought back all those years. She'd just qualified, and it had been one of the first prem births where she'd been midwife in charge. Twins, a complex delivery, and the number of people in the birthing room had made her flustered. Afterwards Oliver had come to the prem nursery to check on his handiwork. The nurse in charge—a dragon of a woman who shot first and asked questions later—had been in the background, as Oliver had unwrapped the blue bundle.

Em had been by his side. She'd gasped and lost colour but Oliver hadn't said a word; hadn't given away by the slightest intake of breath that he'd become aware she'd made a blunder that could have put her job at risk. But the mistake was obvious—the incubators had been brought straight from the birthing suite and were side by side. There was no question who each baby was. Without saying a word, somehow Oliver helped her swap blankets and wristbands and the charge nurse was unaware to this day.

That one action had left her...smitten.

But it hadn't just been his action, she conceded. It had also been the way he'd smiled at her, and then as she'd tried to thank him afterwards, it had been the way he'd laughed it off and told her about dumb things he'd done as a student...and then asked her to have dinner with him...

'I reckon I might like to be a nurse,' Ruby said sleepily. 'You reckon I might?'

'I reckon you're awesome,' Oliver told her. 'I reckon you can do anything you want.'

And then Ruby's eyes flickered closed. The chief anaesthetist gave Oliver a nod—and the operation was under way.

Lightness was put aside.

Oliver had outlined the risks to Ruby—and there were risks. Exposing this tiny baby to the outside world when she was nowhere near ready for birth was so dangerous. Em had no idea how many times it had been done in the past, how successful it had been, but all she knew as she watched was that if it was her baby there was no one she'd rather have behind the scalpel than Oliver.

He was working side by side with Heinz. They

were talking through the procedure together, glancing up every so often at the scans on the screens above their heads, checking positions. They wanted no more of the baby exposed than absolutely necessary.

Another screen showed what they were doing. To Em in the background she could see little of the procedural site but this was being recorded—to be used as Rufus's operation had been—to re-assure another frantic mum?

Please let it have the same result, she pleaded. She was acting as gofer, moving equipment back and forth within reach of the theatre nurse as needed, but she still had plenty of time to watch the screen.

And then the final incision was made. Gently, gently, the baby was rotated within the uterus—and she could see the bulge that was the unsealed spine.

There was a momentary pause as everyone saw it. A collective intake of breath.

'The poor little tacker,' Tristan breathed. 'To be born like that…she'd have had no chance of liv-ing a normal life.'

'Then let's see if we can fix it,' Oliver said in a voice Em had never heard before. And she knew that every nerve was on edge, every last ounce of his skill and Heinz's were at play here.

Please…

The complexity, the minuscule size, the need for accuracy, it was astounding.

Oliver was sweating. Not only was the intensity of his work mind-blowing, but the theatre itself had to be set at a high enough temperature to stop foetal shock.

'Em.' Chris, the chief theatre nurse, called back to her. 'Take over the swabs.'

All hands were needed. Em saw where she, too, was needed. She moved seamlessly into position and acted to stop Oliver's sweat obscuring his vision.

He wasn't aware of her. He wasn't aware of anything.

They were using cameras to blow up the images of the area he and Heinz were working on. Every person there was totally focused on the job or on the screens. Two people at once—two hearts, two lives…

She forgot to breathe. She forgot everything but keeping Oliver's vision clear so he could do what had to be a miracle.

And finally they were closing. Oliver was stitching—maybe his hands were steadier than Heinz's because he was working under instruction. He was inserting what seemed almost microstitches, carefully, carefully manoeuvring the spinal wound closed. Covering the spinal cord and the peripheral nerves. Stopping future damage.

The spine was closed. They were replacing the amniotic fluid. Oliver was closing the uterus, conferring with Heinz, seemingly relaxing a little.

The outer wound was being closed.

The thing was done.

Emily felt like sagging.

She wouldn't. She wiped Oliver's forehead for the final time and at last he had space to turn and give her a smile. To give the whole team a smile. But his smile ended with Em.

'We've done it,' he said with quiet triumph. 'As long as we can keep her on board for another few weeks, we've saved your baby.'

'Your baby'...

Where had that come from?

And then she thought back to the teasing he'd given her when they'd first met, when they'd been working together, she as a brand-new nurse, he as a paediatric surgeon still in training.

'Em, the way you expose your heart... You seem to greet every baby you help deliver as if it's your own,' he'd told her. *'By the end of your career, you'll be like Old Mother Hubbard—or the Pied Piper of Hamelin. Kids everywhere.'*

And wouldn't she just love that! She thought fleetingly of the two she was allowed to love. Gretta and Toby.

She did love them, fiercely, wonderfully, but she looked down at Ruby now and she knew that she had love to spare. Heart on her sleeve or not, she loved this teenage mum, and she loved the little life that was now securely tucked back inside her.

The heart swelled to fit all comers...

She thought back to Oliver's appalling adoptive mother and she thought he'd never known that.

He still didn't know it and they'd gone their separate ways because of it.

She stood back from the table. Her work there was done. She'd wait for Ruby in the recovery ward.

The team had another patient waiting for surgery. Oliver was moving on.

Em already had moved on. She just had to keep moving.

* * *

'Well done.' Out at the sinks the mood was one of quiet but deep satisfaction. There'd be no high fives, not yet—everyone knew the next few days would be critical—but the procedure had gone so smoothly surely they'd avoided embryo shock.

Tristan hitched himself up on the sinks and regarded his friend with satisfaction. He and Oliver had done their general surgical training together. They'd split as Oliver had headed into specialist surgical obstetrics and Tristan into paediatric cardiology, but their friendship was deep and longstanding.

Tristan alone knew the association between Em and Oliver. They'd had one heated discussion about it already...

'The hospital grapevine will find out. Why keep it secret?'

'It's not a secret. It's just a long time ago. Moving on...'

But now...

'Are you telling me you and Em have really moved on?' Tristan demanded as he watched his friend ditch his theatre garb. 'Because, sure, Em's your patient's midwife and she was in Theatre as an observer in that capacity, but the contact you and she had… You might not have been aware how often you flicked her a glance but every time you were about to start something risky, it was like you were looking to her for strength.'

'What the…?' Where had this come from? As if he needed Em for strength? He'd been operating without Em for years.

He'd never depended on her.

'You might say it's in the past,' Tristan went on, inexorably. 'But she's still using your name, and as of today, as an onlooker, it seems to me that the marriage isn't completely over.'

'Will you keep your voice down?' There were nurses and orderlies everywhere.

'You think you can keep this to yourself?'

'It's not obvious.'

'It's obvious,' Tristan said, grinning. 'Midwife Evans and Surgeon Evans. Sparks. The grapevine will go nuts.'

'You're not helping.'

'I'm just observing.' Tristan pushed down from the bench. He and Oliver both had patients waiting. Always there were patients waiting.

'All I'm saying is that I'm interested,' Tristan

said, heading for the door. 'Me and the rest of staff of the Victoria. And some of us are even more interested than others.'

Trained theatre staff were rostered to watch over patients in Recovery, but Isla had cleared the way for Em to stay with Ruby. With no family support, the need to keep Ruby calm was paramount. So Em sat by her bedside and watched. Ruby was drifting lightly towards consciousness, seeming to ease from sedation to natural sleep.

Which might have something to do with the way Em was holding her hand and talking to her.

'It's great, Ruby. You were awesome. Your baby was awesome. It's done, all fixed. Your baby will have the best of chances because of your decision.'

She doubted Ruby could hear her but she said it anyway, over and over, until she was interrupted.

'Hey.' She looked up and Sophia was watching her. Sophia was a partnering midwife, a friend, a woman who had the same fertility issues she did. If there was anyone in this huge staff she was close to, it was Sophia. 'Isla sent me down to see how the op went,' she said, pulling up a chair to sit beside Em. 'All's quiet on the Western Front. We had three nice, normal babies in quick succession this morning and not a sniff of a contraction this arvo. Isla says you can stay here as needed; take as long as you want.'

'We're happy, aren't we, Ruby?' Em said gently, squeezing Ruby's hand, but there was no response. Ruby's natural sleep had grown deeper. 'The operation went brilliantly.' And then, because she couldn't help herself, she added a rider. 'Oliver was brilliant.'

'Yeah, I'd like to talk to you about that,' Sophia said, diffidently now, assessing Ruby as she spoke and realising, as Em had, that there was little chance of Ruby taking in anything she said. 'Rumours are flying. Someone heard Tristan and Oliver talking at the sinks. Evans and Evans. No one's put them together until now. It's a common name. But…Evans isn't your maiden name, is it? Evans is your married name. And according to the rumours, that marriage would be between you and Oliver.'

Whoa. Em flinched. But then…it had to come out sooner or later, she thought. She might as well grit her teeth and confess.

'It was a long time ago,' she murmured. 'We split five years ago but changing my name didn't seem worth the complications. I was Emily Green before. I kind of like Emily Evans better.' She didn't want to say that going to a lawyer, asking for a divorce, had seemed…impossibly final.

'As you kind of like Oliver Evans?' Sophia wiggled down further in her chair, her eyes alight with interest. 'The theatre staff say there were all sorts of sparks between you during the op.'

'Ruby's in my care. Oliver was…keeping me reassured.' But she'd said it too fast, too defensively, and Sophia's eyebrows were hiking.

Drat hospitals and their grapevines, she thought. Actually, they were more than grapevines—they were like Jack's beanstalk. Let one tiny bean out of the can and it exploded to the heavens.

What had Oliver and Tristan been talking about to start this?

And…how was she to stop Sophia's eyebrows hitting the roof?

'You going to tell Aunty Sophia?' she demanded, settling down further in a manner that suggested she was going nowhere until Em did.

'You knew I was married.'

'Yeah, but not to Oliver. Oliver! Em, he's a hunk. And he's already getting a reputation for being one of those rarest of species—a surgeon who can talk to his patients. Honest, Em, he smiled at one of my mums on the ward this morning and my heart flipped. Why on earth...?'

'A smile doesn't make a marriage.' But it did, Em thought miserably. She'd loved that smile. What they'd had...

'So will you tell Aunty Sophia why you split?'

'Kids,' she said brusquely. She'd told Sophia she was infertile but only when Sophia had told her of her own problems. She hadn't elaborated.

'He left you because you couldn't have babies?'

'We...well, I already told you we went through IVF. Cycle upon cycle. What I didn't tell you was that finally I got pregnant. Josh was delivered stillborn at twenty-eight weeks.'

'Oh, Em...' Sophia stared at her in horror. 'You've kept that to yourself, all this time?'

'I don't...talk about it. It hurts.'

'Yeah, well, I can see that,' Sophia said, hopping up to give her friend a resounding hug. 'They say IVF can destroy a marriage—it's so hard. It split you up?'

'The IVF didn't.' Em was remembering the weeks after she'd lost Josh, how close she and Oliver had been, a couple gutted but totally united in their grief. If it hadn't been for Oliver then, she might have gone crazy.

Which had made what had come next even more devastating.

'So what…?'

'I couldn't…do IVF any more,' Em whispered.

Silence.

Ruby seemed soundly asleep. She was still holding the girl's hand. She could feel the strength of Ruby's heartbeat, and the monitors around her told her Ruby's baby was doing fine, as well. The world went on, she thought bleakly, remembering coming out of hospital after losing Josh, seeing all those mums, all those babies…

'Earth to Em,' Sophia said gently at last, and Em hauled herself together and gave her a bleak little smile.

'I wanted a family,' she whispered. 'I think…I was a bit manic after the loss but I was suddenly desperate. Maybe it was an obsession, I don't know, but I told Oliver I wanted to adopt, whatever the cost. And in the end, the cost was him.'

'He didn't want to adopt?'

'He's adopted himself. It wasn't happy, and he wouldn't concede there was another side. He wouldn't risk adoption because he didn't think he could love an adopted kid. And I wasn't prepared to give, either. We were two implacable forces, and there was nowhere to go but to turn away from each other. So there you have it, Sophia. No baby, no marriage. Can I ask you not to talk about it?'

'You don't have to ask,' Sophia said roundly. 'Of course I won't. But this hospital…the walls have ears and what it doesn't know it makes up. Now everyone knows you were married…'

'It'll be a one-day wonder,' Em told her, and then Ruby stirred faintly and her eyes flickered open.

'Well, hi,' Em said, her attention totally now on Ruby. 'Welcome to the other side, Ruby, love. The operation was a complete success. Now all we need to do is let you sleep and let your baby sleep until we're sure you're settled into nice, normal pregnancy again.'

CHAPTER EIGHT

SATURDAY.

Oliver did a morning ward round, walked into Ruby's room—and found Em there.

According to his calculations—and he'd made a few—Em should be off duty. Why was she sitting by Ruby's bedside?

She was darning…a sock?

Both women looked up as he walked in and both women smiled.

'Hey,' Ruby said. 'Is it true? Were you two married?'

'How…?' Em gasped.

'I just heard,' Ruby said blithely. 'It's true, isn't it?'

Em bundled up her needlework and rose—fast. 'Yes,' she managed. 'But it was a long time ago. Sorry, Oliver, I'll be out of your way.'

'Why are you here?' Damn, that had sounded accusatory and he hadn't meant to be.

'I'm off duty but Ruby's teaching me how to darn.'

'That's…important?'

'It is, as a matter of fact,' she said, tossing him a look that might well be described as a glower. And also a warning to keep things light. 'The whole world seems to toss socks away as soon as they get holes. Ruby and I are doing our bit to prevent landfill.'

'Good for you.' He still sounded stiff but he couldn't help it. 'Are you going home now?'

'Yes.'

'So why did you two split?' Ruby was under orders for complete bed rest but she was recovering fast, the bed rest was more for her baby's sake than for hers, and she was obviously aching for diversion.

'Incompatibility,' Em said, trying for lightness, stooping to give Ruby a swift kiss. 'He used to pinch all the bedcovers. He's a huncher—you know the type? He hunches all the covers round him and then rolls in his sleep. I even tried pinning the covers to my side of the bed but I was left with ripped covers and a doomed marriage. I'll pop in tomorrow, Ruby, but meanwhile is there anything you need?'

'More socks?' Ruby said shyly, and Em grinned.

'Ask Dr Evans. I'll bet he has a drawer full. I need to go, Ruby, love. Byee.'

And she was gone.

It had been an informal visit. She'd been wearing jeans and a colourful shirt and her hair was down. She had so much to do at home—he knew she did.

Why was she here on a day off?

Because she cared?

She couldn't stop caring. That had been one of the things he'd loved about her.

He still loved?

'You're still dotty about her,' Ruby said, and he realised he'd been staring at the corridor where she'd disappeared.

'Um…no. Just thinking I've never walked in on a darning lesson before. How's bub?'

'Still kicking.'

'Not too hard?'

'N-no.' And once again he copped that zing of fear.

This was why Em had 'popped in', he thought. This kid was far too alone.

That was Em. She carried her heart on her sleeve.

If it was up to Em they would have adopted, he thought, and, despite the things he'd said to her after Josh had died, he was beginning to accept she was capable of it. *It?* Of loving a child who wasn't her own. The way she'd held Gretta... The way she'd laughed at Toby... Okay, Em was as different from his adoptive mother as it was possible to be, and it had been cruel of him to suggest otherwise.

It had taken him a huge leap of faith to accept that he'd loved Em. Even though he'd supported her through IVF, even though he'd been overjoyed when she'd finally conceived, when Josh had died...

Had a small part of him been relieved? Had a part of him thought he could never extend his heart to all comers?

He would have loved Josh. He did. The morning when they'd sat looking down at the promise that had been their little son had been one of the worst of his life. But the pain that had gone with it…the pain of watching Em's face…

And then for Em to say let's adopt, let's put ourselves up for this kind of pain again for a child he didn't know…

'Let's check your tummy,' he told Ruby, but she was still watching him.

'You are still sweet on her.'

'She's an amazing woman. But as she said, I'm a huncher.'

'Is it because you couldn't have children?'

How…? 'No!'

'It's just, one of the nurses told me Em's got two foster-kids she looks after with her mum. If you and she were married, why didn't you have your own?'

'Ruby, I think you have quite enough to think about with your own baby, without worrying about other people's,' he said, mock sternly.

'You're saying butt out?'

'And let me examine you. Yes.'

'Yes, Doctor,' she said, mock meekly, but she managed the beginnings of a cheeky grin. 'But you can't tell me to butt out completely. It seemed no one in this hospital knew you guys have been

married. So now everyone in this hospital is really, really interested. Me, too.'

After that he was really ambivalent about the baby-
sitting he'd promised. Actually, he'd been pretty
ambivalent in the first place. Work was zooming
to speed with an intensity that was staggering.
He could easily ring and say he was needed at the
hospital and it wouldn't have been a lie.

But he'd promised, so he put his head down and
worked and by a quarter to one he was pulling up
outside the place Em called home.

Em was in the front yard, holding Toby on a
push-along tricycle. When she saw him she swung
Toby up into her arms and waved.

Toby hesitated a moment—and then waved, too.

The sight took him aback. He paused before getting out of the car. He knew Em was waiting for
him, but he needed a pause to catch his breath.

This was the dream. They'd gone into their marriage expecting this—love, togetherness, family.

He'd walked away so that Em could still have it.
The fact that she'd chosen to do it alone…

But she wasn't alone. She had her mum. She

had Mike next door and his brood. She had great friends at the hospital.

The only one missing from the picture was him, and the decision to walk away had been his.

If he'd stayed, though, they wouldn't have had any of this. They'd be a professional couple, absorbed in their work and their social life.

How selfish was that? The certainties of five years ago were starting to seem just a little bit wobbly.

'Hey, are you stuck to the seat?' Em was carrying Toby towards him, laughing at him. She looked younger today, he thought. Maybe it was the idea that she was about to have some free time. An afternoon with her mum.

She was about to have some time off from kids who weren't her own.

But they were her own. Toby had his arms wrapped around her, snuggling into her shoulder.

He had bare feet. Em was tickling his toes as she walked, making him giggle.

She loved these kids.

He'd thought… Okay, he'd thought he was being selfless, walking away five years ago. He'd been giving up his marriage so Em could have what she wanted. Now… Why was he now feeling the opposite? Completely, utterly selfish?

Get a grip, he told himself. He was here to work.

'Your babysitter's here, ma'am,' he said, finally climbing from the car. 'All present and correct.'

She was looking ruefully at the car. 'Still the hire car? Can't you get parts?'

'They're hard to come by.' He'd spent hours on the internet tracking down the parts he needed.

'Oh, Ollie…'

No one called him Ollie.

Em did.

She put her hand on his arm and he thought, She's comforting me because of a wrecked car. And she's coping with kids with wrecked lives…

How to make a rat feel an even bigger rat.

But her sympathy was real. Everything about her was real, he thought. Em… He'd loved this woman.

He loved this woman?

'Hey, will you go with Uncle Ollie?' Em was saying, moving on, prising Toby away from his neck-hugging. 'I bet he knows how to tickle toes, too.'

'I can tickle toes.' He was a paediatric surgeon. He could keep a kid entertained.

But Toby caught him unawares. He twisted in Em's arms and launched himself across, so fast Oliver almost didn't catch him. Em grabbed, Oliver grabbed and suddenly they were in a sandwich hug, with Toby sandwiched in the middle.

Toby gave a muffled chortle, like things had gone exactly to plan. Which, maybe in Toby's world, they had.

But he had so much wrong with him. His tiny spine was bent; he'd have operation after operation in front of him, years in a brace...

He'd have Em.

He should pull away, but Em wasn't pulling away. For this moment she was holding, hugging, as if she needed it. As if his hug was giving her something...

Something that, as his wife, had once been her right?

'Em...'

But the sound of his voice broke the moment. She tugged away, flipped an errant curl behind her ear, tried to smile.

'Sorry. I should expect him to do that—he does it all the time with Mike. He has an absolute conviction that the grown-ups in his life are to be trusted never, ever to drop him, and so far it's paid off. One day, though, Toby, lad, you'll find out what the real world's like.'

'But you'll shield him as long as you can.'

'With every ounce of power I possess,' she said simply. 'But, meanwhile, Mum's ready to go. She's so excited she didn't sleep last night. Gretta's fed. Everything's ready, all I need to do is put on clean jeans and comb my hair.'

'Why don't you put on a dress?' he asked, feeling...weird. Out of kilter. This was none of his business, but he was starting to realise just how important this afternoon was to Em and her mum. And how rare. 'Make it a special occasion.'

'Goodness, Oliver, I don't think I've worn a dress for five years,' she flung at him over her shoulder as she headed into the house. 'Why would the likes of me need a dress?'

And he thought of the social life they'd once had. Did she miss it? he wondered, but he tickled Toby's toes, the little boy giggled and he knew that she didn't.

* * *

They left fifteen minutes later, like a pair of jail escapees, except that they were escapees making sure all home bases were covered. Their 'jail' was precious.

'Mike might come over later to collect Toby,' Em told him. 'Toby loves Mike, so if he does that's fine by us. That'll mean you only have Gretta so you should cope easily. You have both our cellphone numbers? You know where everything is? And Gretta needs Kanga...if she gets upset, Kanga can fix her. But don't let her get tired. If she has trouble breathing you can raise her oxygen...'

'Em, trust me, I'm a doctor,' he said, almost pushing them out the door.

'And you have how much experience with kids?'

'I'm an obstetrician and a surgeon.'

'My point exactly. Here they're outside their mum, not inside, and you don't have an anaesthetist to put them to sleep. There's a stack of movies ready to play. You can use the sandpit, too. Gretta loves it, but you need to keep her equipment sand-free...'

'Em, go,' he said, exasperated. 'Adrianna, take

Em's arm and pull. Em, trust me. You can, you know.'

'I do know that,' Em told him, and suddenly she darted back across the kitchen and gave him a swift kiss on the cheek. It was a thank-you kiss, a perfunctory kiss, and why it had the power to burn... 'I always have,' she said simply. 'You're a very nice man, Oliver Evans. I would have trusted you to be a great dad, even if you couldn't trust yourself. That's water under the bridge now, but I still trust you, even if it's only for an afternoon.'

And she blinked a couple of times—surely they weren't tears?—then ducked back and kissed Gretta once again—and she was gone.

And Oliver was left with two kids.

And silence.

The kids were watching him. Toby was in his arms, leaning back to gaze into his eyes. Cautiously assessing? Gretta was sitting in an over-sized pushchair, surrounded by cushions.

To trust or not to trust?

Toby's eyes were suddenly tear-filled. A couple of fat tears tracked down his face.

Gretta just stared at him, her face expression-less. Waiting to see what happened next?

Both were silent.

These were damaged kids, he thought. Re-jects. They'd be used to a life where they were left. They'd come from parents who couldn't or wouldn't care for them and they had significant medical problems. They'd be used to a life where hospital stays were the norm. They weren't kids who opened their mouths and screamed whenever they were left.

Could you be stoic at two and at four? That's how they seemed. Stoic.

It was a bit…gut-wrenching.

Kanga—it must be Kanga: a chewed, bedrag-gled, once blue stuffed thing with long back paws and a huge tail—was lying on the table. He picked it—him?—up and handed him to Toby. Gretta watched with huge eyes. This wasn't what was supposed to happen, her eyes said. This was *her* Kanga.

He lifted Gretta out of her chair with his spare arm and carried both kids out into the yard, under the spreading oak at the bottom of the garden where the lawn was a bit too long, lushly green.

He set both kids down on the grass. Fuzzy the dog flopped down beside them. He, too, seemed wary.

Toby was still holding Kanga. Warily.

He tugged Gretta's shoes off so both kids had bare feet. Em had made the tickling thing work. Maybe it'd work for him.

He took Kanga from Toby, wriggled him slowly towards Gretta's toes—and ticked Gretta's toes with Kanga's tail.

Then, as both kids looked astonished, he bounced Kanga across to Toby and tickled his.

Toby looked more astonished. He reached out to grab Kanga, but Oliver was too fast. The tickling tail went back to Gretta's toes—and then, as Toby reached further, Kanga bounced sideways and tickled Fuzzy on the nose.

Fuzzy opened his mouth to grab but Kanga boinged back to Gretta, this time going from one foot to the other.

And then, as Gretta finally reacted, Kanga boinged up and touched her nose—and then bounced back to Toby.

Toby stared down in amazement at his toes

being tickled and his eyes creased, the corners of his mouth twitched—and he chuckled.

It was a lovely sound but it wasn't enough. Kanga bounced back to Gretta, kissed her nose again, then bounced right on top of Fuzzy's head.

Fuzzy leaped to his feet and barked.

Kanga went back to Toby's toes.

And finally, finally, and it was like a minor miracle all by itself, Gretta's serious little face relaxed. She smiled and reached out her hand.

'Kanga,' she said, and Kanga flew to her hand. She grabbed him and held, gazing dotingly at her beloved blue thing.

'Kanga,' she said again, and she opened her fingers—and held Kanga back out to Oliver.

Her meaning was clear. He's mine but it's okay to play. In fact, she wanted to play.

But that one word had left her breathless. What the...? He'd seen the levels of oxygen she was receiving and she was still breathless? But she was still game.

She was trusting.

He wanted to hug her.

She was four years old. He'd met her twice. He was feeling...feeling...

'Hey!' It was Mike, and thank heaven for Mike. He was getting emotional and how was a man to keep tickling when he was thinking of what was in store for this little girl? He looked across at the gate and smiled at Mike with gratitude.

'Hey, yourself.'

'We're going to the beach,' Mike called. 'You want to come?'

'I'm sitting the kids,' he said, and Mike looked at him like he was a moron.

'Yeah. Kid-sitting. Beach. It's possible to combine them—and your two love the beach. Katy and Drew are staying home—Katy's still under the weather but her mum's here and Drew has a mate over. But we have four kid seats in the wagon—we always seem to have a spare kid— and why not?'

Why not? Because he'd like to stay lying under the tree, tickling toes?

It wouldn't last. His child entertainment range was limited, to say the least, and both kids were looking eager.

But, Gretta... Sand... Maybe he could sort it.

'What if we put one of the car seats into your car,' Mike said, eyeing the rental car parked at the kerb. 'Rental cars always have bolts to hold 'em. That way you can follow me and if Gretta gets tired you can bring her straight home. And we have beach shelters for shade. We have so much beach gear I feel like a pack mule going up and down the access track. Katy's mum's packed afternoon tea. Coming?'

'Yeah,' he said, because there was nothing else he could say. But there was part of him that was thinking as he packed up and prepared to take his charges beachwards, I wouldn't have minded caring for them myself. I wouldn't have minded proving that I could be a...

A father? By minding them for a couple of hours? Would that make him a hero? Could it even disprove what he'd always felt—that you couldn't love a kid who wasn't your own? Of course it couldn't.

It was just that, as the kids had chuckled, he'd felt, for one sliver of a crazy moment, that he could have been completely wrong. That maybe his judgement five years ago had been clouded, distorted by his own miserable childhood.

And an afternoon alone with these kids would prove what? Nothing. He'd made a choice five years ago. It had been the only honest option, and nothing had changed.

Except the way Gretta was smiling at the thought of the beach seemed to be changing things, like it or not. And the knowledge that Em would think giving Gretta an afternoon at the beach was great.

Would it make Em smile?

'You coming, mate, or are you planning on writing a thesis on the pros and cons?' Mike demanded, and he caught himself and took Kanga from Toby and handed him to Gretta.

'We're coming,' he told him. He looked at the muscled hulk of a tattooed biker standing at the gate and Oliver Evans, specialist obstetric surgeon, admitted his failings. 'But you might need to help me plan what to take. I'm a great obstetrician but as a father I'm the pits.'

'You reckon he'll be okay? You reckon he'll manage?'

'If you're worried, ring Mike.'

Em and her mum were lying on adjoining massage tables. They had five minutes' 'down' time before the massage was to begin. The soft, cushioned tables were gently warmed, the lights were dim, the sound of the sea washed through the high windows and a faint but lovely perfume was floating from the candles in the high-set sconces.

They should almost be asleep already but Em couldn't stop fretting.

'Ring Mike and ask him to check,' Adrianna said again. 'We all want you to enjoy this. I want to enjoy this. Check.'

So she rang. She lay on her gorgeous table and listened to Mike's growl.

'You're not supposed to be worrying. Get back to doing nothing.'

'You've got Toby?'

'Me and Oliver—that's one hell of a name, isn't it?—we're gunna have to think of something shorter—have Toby—and my kids and Gretta. We're at the beach. Want to see? I'm sending a video. Watch it and then shut up, Em. Quit it with your worrying. Me and your Ollie have things in hand.'

He disconnected. She stared at the phone, feeling disconcerted. Strange. That her kids were somewhere else without her... With Oliver. Ollie...

No one called him Ollie except her, but now

Mike was doing the same. It was like two parts of her life were merging.

The old and the new?

It was her imagination. Oliver…Ollie?…would do this afternoon of childminding and move on.

A ping announced the arrival of a message. She clicked and sure enough there was a video, filmed on Mike's phone and sent straight through.

There was Toby with Mike's two littlies. They were building a sandcastle—sort of. It was a huge mound of sand, covered with seaweed and shells. Fuzzy was digging a hole on the far side and Mike's bitser dog was barking in excitement.

As Em watched, Toby picked up a bucket of water and spilt it over the castle—and chuckled. Mike laughed off camera.

'If you think I don't have anything better to do than fill buckets for you, young Toby—you're right…'

And then the camera panned away, down to the shoreline—and Em drew in her breath.

For there was Oliver—and Gretta.

They were sitting on the wet sand, where the low, gentle waves were washing in, washing out.

Oliver had rigged a beach chair beside them, wedging it secure with something that looked like sandbags. Wet towels filled with sand?

Gretta's oxygen cylinder was high on the seat, safe from the shallow inrushes of water, but Ollie and Gretta were sitting on the wet sand.

He had Gretta on his knee. They were facing the incoming waves, waiting for one to reach them.

'Here it comes,' Oliver called, watching as a wave broke far out. 'Here it comes, Gretta, ready or not. One, two, three...'

And he swung Gretta back against his chest, hugging her as the water surrounded them, washing Gretta's legs, swishing around his body.

He was wearing board shorts. He was naked from the waist up.

She'd forgotten his body...

No, she hadn't. Her heart couldn't clench like this if she'd forgotten.

'More,' Gretta whispered, wriggling her toes in the water, twisting so she could see the wave recede. Her eyes were sparkling with delight. She was so close to the other side, this little one, and yet for now she was just a kid having fun.

A kid secure with her... Her what?

Her friend. With Oliver, who couldn't give his heart.

Silently Em handed her phone to her mum and waited until Adrianna had seen the video.

Adrianna sniffed. 'Oh, Em...'

'Yeah.'

'Do you think...?'

'No.'

'It's such a shame.'

'It's the way it is,' Em said bleakly. 'But...but for now, he's making Gretta happy.'

'He's lovely,' Adrianna said stoutly.

'Don't I know it?' Em whispered. 'Don't I wish I didn't?'

'Em...'

The door opened. Their massage ladies entered, silently, expecting their clients to be well on the way on their journey to complete indulgence.

'Are you ready?' the woman due to massage Em asked. 'Can you clear your mind of every-thing past, of everything future and just let yourself be. For now there should be nothing outside this room.'

But there was, Em thought as skilful hands started their skin-tingling work. There was a vision of her ex-husband holding her little girl. Making Gretta happy.

Massages were wonderful, she decided as her body responded to the skill of the woman working on her.

They might be wonderful but thinking about Oliver was...better?

He sat in the waves and watched—and felt—Gretta enjoy herself. She was a wraith of a child, a fragile imp, dependent on the oxygen that sustained her, totally dependent on the adults who cared for her.

She trusted him. She faced the incoming waves with joy because she was absolutely sure Oliver would lift her just in time, protect the breathing tube, hug her against his body, protect her from all harm.

But harm was coming to this little one, and there was nothing anyone could do about it. He'd mentioned Gretta to Tristan and Tristan had spelt out the prognosis. With so much deformity of the heart, it was a matter of time…

Not very much time.

That he had this time with her today was precious. He didn't know her, she wasn't his kid, but, regardless, it was gold.

If he could somehow take the pain away…

He couldn't. He couldn't protect Gretta.

He couldn't protect Em.

Hell, but he wanted to. And not just for Em, he conceded. For this little one. This little girl who laughed and twisted and buried her face in his shoulder and then turned to face the world again.

Em loved her. *Loved her.*

An adopted child.

He'd thought… Yeah, okay, he knew. If Em was able to have her own child it'd all change. Gretta would take second place.

But did he know? Five years ago he'd been sure. He'd been totally judgmental and his marriage was over because of it.

Now the sands were shifting. He was shifting.

'More,' Gretta ordered, and he realised two small waves had washed over her feet and he hadn't done the lift and squeal routine. Bad.

'Em wouldn't forget,' he told Gretta as he lifted and she squealed. 'Em loves you.'

But Gretta's face was buried in his shoulder, and that question was surfacing—again. Over and over.

Had he made the mistake of his life?

Could he...?

Focus on Gretta, he told himself. Anything else was far too hard.

Anything else was far too soon.

Or five years too late?

CHAPTER NINE

BY THE TIME Em and Adrianna arrived home, Oliver had the kids squeaky clean. He'd bathed them, dressed them in their PJs, tidied the place as best he could and was feeling extraordinarily smug about his child-minding prowess.

The kids were tired but happy. All Em and Adrianna had to do was feed them and tuck them into bed. He could leave. Job done.

They walked in looking glowing. They both had beautifully styled, shiny hair. They both looked as squeaky clean as the kids—scrubbed? They'd obviously shopped a little.

Em was wearing a new scarf in bright pink and muted greens. It made her look…how Em used to look, he thought. Like a woman who had time to think about her appearance. Free?

And impressed.

'Wow.' Both women were gazing around the kitchen in astonishment. The kids were in their chairs at the table. Oliver had just started making toast to keep them going until dinner. 'Wow,' Adrianna breathed again. 'There's not even a mess.'

'Mike took them all to the beach,' Em reminded her, but she was smiling at Oliver, her eyes thanking him.

'Hey, I had to clean the bathroom,' Oliver said, mock wounded. 'I've had to do some work.'

'Of course you have.' Adrianna flopped onto the nearest chair. 'Hey, if we make some eggs we could turn that toast into soldiers, and the kids' dinner is done. Kids, how about if I eat egg and toast soldiers too, and then I'll flop into bed, as well. I'm pooped.' But then she turned thoughtful. 'But, Em, you aren't ready for bed yet. You look fabulous, the night's still young, the kids are good and Oliver's still here. Why don't you two go out to dinner?'

Em stared at her like she'd lost her mind. 'Dinner…'

'You know, that thing you eat at a restaurant. Or maybe it could be fish and chips overlooking the bay. It's a gorgeous night. Oliver, do you have anything else on?'

'No, but—'

'Then go on, the two of you. You know you want to.'

'Mum, we don't want to.'

'Really?' Adrianna demanded. 'Honestly? Look at me, Em, and say you really don't want to go out to dinner with Oliver. Oliver, you do the same.'

Silence.

'There you go, then,' she said, satisfied. 'Off you go. Shoo.'

What else could they do but follow instructions? The night was warm and still, a combination unusual for Melbourne, where four seasons were often famously represented in one day. But this night the gods were smiling. Even the fish-and-chip kiosk didn't have too long a queue. Oliver ordered, then he and Em walked a block back from the beach to buy a bottle of wine, and returned just as their order was ready.

They used to do this often, Em thought. Once upon a time...

'I still have our picnic rug,' Oliver said ruefully, as they collected their feast. 'But it's in the back of the Morgan.'

'I'm sorry.'

'Don't be. Just be glad your wagon only got scratches—you're the one who's dependent on it. Moving on... Hey, how about this?' A family was just leaving an outside table and it was pretty much in the best position on the beachfront. Oliver swooped on it before a bunch of teenagers reached it, spread his parcels over it and signalled her to come. Fast.

'You're worse than the seagulls,' she retorted, smiling at his smug expression. 'Talk about swoop for the kill...'

'Table-swooping's one of my splinter skills,' he told her. 'Surely you remember.'

'I try...not to.'

'Does that help? Trying not to?'

Silence. She couldn't think of an answer. They unwrapped their fish and chips and ate a few. They watched a couple of windsurfers trying to guide their kites across the bay with not enough breeze, but the question still hung.

How soon could you forget a marriage? Never? It was never for her.

'I... How was America?' she asked at last, because she had to say something, the silence was becoming oppressive.

'Great. I learned so much.'

'You went away an obstetrician and came back...'

'I'm still first and foremost an obstetrician.'

'But you have the skills to save Ruby's baby—and countless others. You must feel it's worth it.'

'Em...'

'And you wouldn't have done that if we'd stayed together.' She was determined to get this onto some sort of normal basis, where they could talk about their marriage as if it was just a blip in their past. It was nothing that could affect their future. 'But I'm surprised you haven't met anyone else.' She hesitated but then ploughed on. She needed to say this. Somehow.

'You ached to be a dad,' she whispered, because somehow saying it aloud seemed wrong. 'I thought... There's nothing wrong with you. It's me who has the fertility problems. I thought you'd have met someone else by now and organised our divorce. Isn't that why we split? I sort of...I sort of wanted to think of you married with a couple of kids.'

'Did you really want that?' His curt response startled her into splashing her wine. She didn't want it anyway, she decided. She put down her glass with care and met his look head-on.

Say it like it is.

'That's what you wanted. That's why I agreed to separate.'

'I thought ending the marriage was all about you needing a partner so you could adopt.'

'It's true I wanted kids,' she managed, and her voice would hardly work for her. It was hard even to whisper. 'But I never wanted another husband than you.'

'You didn't want me.'

'Your terms were too hard, Oliver. Maybe now…maybe given some space it might be different. But we'd lost Josh and I was so raw, so needy. All I wanted was a child to hold… I think maybe I was a little crazy. I demanded too much of you. I hadn't realised quite how badly you'd been wounded.'

'I hadn't been wounded.'

'I've met your adoptive parents, remember? I've met your appalling brother.'

'I'm well over that.'

'Do you ever get over being not wanted? You were adopted, seemingly adored, and then suddenly supplanted by your parents' "real" son. I can't imagine how much that must have hurt.'

'It's past history.'

'It's not,' she said simply. 'Because it affects who you are. It always will. Maybe...' She hesitated but this had been drifting in and out of her mind for five years now. Was it better left unsaid? Maybe it was, but she'd say it anyway. 'Maybe it will affect any child you have, adopted or not. Maybe that's why you haven't moved on. Would you have loved Josh, Oliver, or would you have resented him because he'd have had the love you never had?'

'That's nuts.'

'Yeah? So why not organise a divorce? Why not remarry?'

'Because of you,' he said, before he could stop himself. 'Because I still love you.'

She stilled. The whole night seemed to still.

There were people on the foreshore, people on the beach. The queue to the fish-and-chip shop was right behind them. Kids were flying by on their skateboards. Mums and dads were pushing strollers.

Because I still love you...

He reached out and touched her hand lightly, his lovely surgeon's fingers tracing her work-worn skin. She spent too much time washing, she thought absently. She should use more moisturiser. She should...

Stop blathering. This was too important.

Five years ago they'd walked away from each other. Had it all been some ghastly mistake? Could they just...start again?

'Em...' He rose and came round to her side of the table. His voice was urgent now. Pressing home a point? He sat down beside her, took both her hands in his and twisted her to face him. 'Do you feel it, too?'

Did she feel it? How could she not? She'd married this man. She'd loved him with all her heart. She'd borne him a son.

He was holding her, and his hold was strong and compelling. His gaze was on her, and on her alone.

A couple of seagulls, sensing distraction, landed on the far side of the table and edged towards the fish-and-chip parcel. They could take what they liked, she thought. This moment was too important.

Oliver... Her husband...

'Em,' he said again, and his hold turned to a tug. He tugged her as he'd tugged her a thousand times before, as she'd tugged him, as their mutual need meant an almost instinctive coming together of two bodies.

Her face lifted to his—once again instinctively, because this was her husband. She was a part of him, and part of her had never let go. Never thought of letting go.

And his mouth was on hers and he was kissing her and the jolty, nervy, pressurised, outside world faded to absolutely nothing.

There was only Oliver. There was only this moment.

There was only this kiss.

She melted into him—of course she did. Her body had spent five years loving this man and it responded now as if it had once again found its true north. Warmth flooded through her—no, make that heat. Desire, strength and surety.

This man was her home.

This man was her heart.

Except he wasn't. The reasons they'd split were still there, practical, definite, and even though she was surrendering herself to the kiss—how could she not?—there was still a part of her brain that refused to shut down. Even though her body was all his, even though she was returning his kiss with a passion that matched his, even though her hands were holding him as if she still had the right to hold, that tiny part was saying this was make-believe.

This was a memory of times past.

This would hurt even more when it was over. Tug away now.

But she couldn't. He was holding her as if she was truly loved. He was kissing her regardless of the surroundings, regardless of the wolf whistles coming from the teenagers at the next table, regardless of…what was true.

It didn't matter. She needed this kiss. She needed this man.

And then the noise surrounding them suddenly grew. The whistles stopped and became hoots of laughter. There were a couple of warning cries and finally, finally, they broke apart to see…

Their fish...

While they had been otherwise...engaged, seagulls had sneaked forward, grabbing chips from the edge of their unwrapped parcel. Now a couple of braver ones had gone further.

They'd somehow seized the edge of one of their pieces of fish, and dragged it free of the packaging. They'd hauled it out...and up.

There were now five gulls...no, make that six... each holding an edge of the fish fillet. The fish was hovering in the air six feet above them while the gulls fought for ownership. They'd got it, but now they all wanted to go in different directions.

The rest of the flock had risen, too, squawking around them, waiting for the inevitable catastrophe and broken pieces.

Almost every person around them had stopped to look, and laugh, at the flying fish and at the two lovers who'd been so preoccupied that they hadn't even defended their meal.

A couple more gulls moved in for the kill and the fish almost spontaneously exploded. Bits of fish went everywhere.

Oliver grabbed the remaining parcel, scooping it up before the scraps of flying fish hit, and shooed the gulls away. They were now down to half their chips and only one piece of fish, but he'd saved the day. The crowd hooted their delight, and Oliver grinned, but Em wasn't thinking about fish and chips, no matter how funny the drama.

How had that happened? It was like they'd been teenagers again, young lovers, so caught up in each other that the world hadn't existed.

But the world did exist.

'I believe I've saved most of our feast,' Oliver said ruefully, and she smiled, but her smile was forced. The world was steady again, her real world. For just a moment she'd let herself be drawn into history, into fantasy. Time to move on…

'We need to concentrate on what's happening now,' she said.

'We do.' He was watching her, his lovely brown eyes questioning. He always could read her, Em thought, suddenly resentful. He could see things about her she didn't know herself.

But he'd kept himself to himself. She'd been married to him for five years and she hadn't known the depth of feeling he'd had about his childhood until the question of adoption had come up. She'd met his adoptive parents, she'd known

they were awful, but Oliver had treated them—
and his childhood—with light dismissal.

'They raised me, they gave me a decent start, I
got to be a doctor and I'm grateful.'

But he wasn't. In those awful few weeks after
losing Josh, when she'd finally raised adoption
as an option, his anger and his grief had shocked
them both. It had resonated with such depth and
fury it had torn them apart.

So, no, she didn't know this man. Not then. Not
now.

And kissing him wasn't going to make it one
whit better.

He'd said he still loved her. Ten years ago he'd
said that, too, and yet he'd walked away, telling
her to move on. Telling her to find someone else
who could fit in with her dreams.

'Em, I'd like to—'

'Have your fish before it gets cold or gets snaf-
fled by another bird?' She spoke too fast, rushing
in before he could say anything serious, anything
that matched the look on his face that said his
emotions were all over the place. That said the
kiss had done something for him that matched

the emotions she was feeling. That said their marriage wasn't over?

But it was over, she told herself fiercely. She'd gone through the pain of separation once and there was no way she was going down that path again. Love? The word itself was cheap, she thought. Their love had been tested, and found wanting. 'That's what I need to do,' she added, still too fast, and took a chip and ate it, even though hunger was the last thing on her mind right now. 'I need to eat fast and get back to the kids. Oliver, that kiss was an aberration. We need to forget it and move on.'

'Really?'

'Really. Have a chip before we lose the lot.'

The kids were asleep when she got home, and so was Adrianna. The house was in darkness. Oliver swung out of the driver's seat as if he meant to accompany her to the door, but she practically ran.

'I need my bed, Oliver. Goodnight.'

He was still watching her as she closed the front door. She'd been rude, she admitted as she headed for the children's bedroom. He'd given her a day out, a day off. If he'd been a stranger she would have spent time thanking him.

She should still thank him.

Except…he'd kissed her. He'd said he loved her.

She stood in the kids' bedroom, between the two cots, watching them sleeping in the dim light cast by a Humpty Dumpty figure that glowed a soft pink to blue and then back again.

She had to work with him, she reminded herself. She needed to get things back to a formal footing, fast.

Resolute, she grabbed her phone and texted.

Thank you for today. It was really generous. The kiss was a mistake but I dare say the gulls are grateful. And Mum and I are grateful, too.

That's what was needed, she thought. Make it light. Put the gratitude back to the plural—herself and her mother—and the seagulls? She was thanking someone she'd once known for a generous gesture.

Only…was it more than that? Surely.

He'd kissed her. Her fingers crept involuntarily to her mouth. She could still feel him, she thought. She could still taste him.

After five years, her body hadn't forgotten him. Her body still wanted him.

He'd said he still loved her.

Had she been crazy to walk away from him all those years ago? Her body said yes, but here in this silent house, listening to the breathing of two children who'd become her own, knowing clearly and bleakly where they'd be if she hadn't taken them in, she could have no regrets. Her mind didn't.

It was only her heart and her body that said something else entirely.

What he wanted to do was stand outside and watch the house for a while. Why? Because it felt like his family was in there.

That was a dumb thought. He'd laid down his ultimatum five years ago and he'd moved on. He'd had five professionally satisfying years getting the skills he needed to be one of the world's top in-utero surgeons. Babies lived now because of him. He'd never have had that chance if he'd stayed here—if he'd become part of Em's menagerie.

He couldn't stay standing outside the house, like a stalker, like someone creepy. What he'd like was to take his little Morgan for a long drive along the coast. The car was like his balm, his escape.

Em had smashed his car. She'd also smashed... something else.

She'd destroyed the equilibrium he'd built around himself over the last few years. She'd destroyed the fallacy that said he was a loner; that said he didn't need anyone.

He wanted her. Fiercely, he wanted her. He'd kissed her tonight and it would have been worth all the fish.

It had felt right.

It had felt like he'd been coming home.

His phone pinged and he flipped it open. Em's polite thank-you note greeted him, and he snapped it shut.

She was making light of the kiss. Maybe that was wise.

Dammit, he couldn't keep standing here. Any moment now she'd look out the window and see him. Ex-husband loitering...

He headed back to the hire car. He had an apartment at the hospital but he wasn't ready for sleep yet. Instead, he headed back to the beach.

He parked, got rid of his shoes and walked along the sand.

The night was still and warm. This evening the beach had been filled with families, kids whooping it up, soaking up the last of Melbourne's summer, but now the beach seemed to be the domain of couples. Couples walking hand in hand in the shallows. Couples lying on rugs on the sand, holding each other.

Young loves?

He walked on and passed a couple who looked to be in their seventies, maybe even older. They were walking slowly. The guy had a limp, a gammy hip? The woman was holding his hand as if she was supporting him.

But the hold wasn't one of pure physical support, he thought. Their body language said they'd been holding each other for fifty years.

He wanted it still. So badly...

Could he take on the kids? Could he take that risk?

Was it a risk? He'd held Gretta today and what he'd felt...

She had Down's syndrome with complications. Tristan said her life expectancy could be measured in months. It was stupid—impossible even—to give your heart to such a kid.

He could still hear his adoptive mother…

'It's not like he's really ours. If we hadn't had Brett then we wouldn't have known what love really is. And now…we're stuck with him. It's like we have a cuckoo in the nest…'

If he ever felt like that…

It was too hard. He didn't know how to feel.

But Em had made the decision for him. She'd moved on, saying he was free to find someone and have kids of his own. Kids who he could truly love.

Hell. He raked his hair and stared out at the moonlit water.

Melbourne's bay was protected. The waves were small, even when the weather was wild, but on a night like this they were practically non-existent. The windsurfers had completely run out of wind. The moonlight was a silver shimmer over the sea and the night seemingly an endless reflection of the starlit sky.

He wanted Em with him.

He wanted her to be…free?

It wasn't going to happen. She had encumbrances. No, he thought, she has people she loves. Kids. Her mother.

Not him.

It's for the best, he thought, shoving his hands deep into his pockets and practically glaring at the moon. I should never have come to the Victoria. I wouldn't have if I'd known Em would be here.

So leave?

Maybe he would, he thought. He'd agreed with Charles Delamere on a three-month trial.

Twelve weeks to go?

CHAPTER TEN

ON MONDAY OLIVER hit the wards early. He'd been in the day before, not because he'd been on duty but because he'd wanted to check on Ruby. But Ruby was doing all the right things and so was her baby, so he didn't check her first. He worked on the things he needed for his embryonic research lab, then decided to check the midwives' roster and choose a time to visit Ruby when he knew Em wouldn't be around.

So he headed—surreptitiously, he thought—to the nurses' station in the birthing centre—just as Isla Delamere came flying down the corridor, looking, for Isla, very harassed indeed.

When she saw Oliver she practically sagged in relief.

'Dr Evans. Oliver. I know your specialty's in-utero stuff and I know Charles has said you can spend the rest of your time on your research but you're an obstetrician first and foremost, yes?'

'Yes.' Of course he was.

'I have four births happening and we're stretched. Two are problems. Emily's coping with one, I have the other. Mine's a bit of a spoilt socialite—she was booked at a private hospital but had hysterics at the first labour pain so her husband's brought her here because we're closer. I can deal with that. But Em's looking after a surrogate mum. She's carrying her sister's child—her sister's egg, her sister's husband's sperm, all very organised—but the emotion in there seems off the planet. Maggie's a multigravida, four kids of her own, no trouble with any, but now she's slowed right down and her sister's practically hysterical. But we can't kick her out. Oliver, Em needs support. Our registrar's off sick, Darcie's at a conference, Sean's coping with a Caesar so that leaves you. Can you help?'

'Of course.'

'Excellent. Here are the case notes. Suite Four.'

'You're okay with yours?'

'My one wants pethidine, morphine, spinal blocks, amputation at the waist, an immediate airlift to Hawaii and her body back,' Isla said grimly. 'And she's only two centimetres dilated. Heaven help us when it's time to push. But I've coped with worse than this in my time. What Em's coping with seems harder. She needs you, Dr Evans. Go.'

The last time he'd seen her he'd kissed her. Now...

Em seemed to be preparing to do a vaginal examination. She was scrubbed, dressed in theatre gear, looking every inch a midwife. Every inch a professional. And the look she gave him as he slipped into the room had nothing to do with the kiss, nothing to do with what was between them. It was pure, professional relief.

'Here's Dr Evans,' she said briskly to the room in general. 'He's one of our best obstetricians. You're in good hands now, Maggie.'

'She doesn't need to be in good hands.' A woman who looked almost the mirror image of the woman in the bed—except that she was smartly dressed, not a hair out of place, looking like she was about to step into a boardroom—was edging round the end of the bed to see what Em was doing. She ignored Oliver. 'Maggie, you just need to push. Thirty-six hours... You can do this. It's taking too long. Just push.'

Em cast him a beseeching look—and he got it in one. The whole set-up.

A guy who was presumably Maggie's husband was sitting beside her, holding her hand. He looked almost as stressed as his labouring wife.

The other woman had a guy with her, as well, presumably her husband, too? He was dressed in casual chinos and a cashmere sweater. Expensive. Smooth.

Both he and his wife seemed focused on where the action should be taking place. Where their child would be born. Even though the woman had been talking to Maggie, she'd been looking at the wrong end of the bed.

Surrogate parenthood... Oliver had been present for a couple of those before, and he'd found the emotion involved was unbelievable. Surrogacy for payment was illegal in this country. It had to be a gift, and what a gift! To carry a child for your sister...

But Maggie wasn't looking as if she was thinking of gifts. She was looking beyond exhaustion.

Thirty-six hours...

'Can't you push?' Maggie's sister said again, fretfully. 'Come on, Maggie, with all of yours it was over in less than twelve hours. The book says it should be faster for later pregnancies. You can do it. You have to try.'

'Maggie needs to go at her own pace,' Em said, in a tone that told him she'd said it before, possibly a lot more than once. 'This baby will come when she's ready.'

'But all she needs to do is push...'

He'd seen enough. He'd heard enough. Oliver looked at Maggie's face, and that of her husband. He looked at Em and saw sheer frustration and he moved.

'Tell me your names,' he said, firmly, cutting off the woman who looked about to issue another order. 'Maggie, I already know yours. Who are the rest of you?'

'I'm Rob,' said the man holding Maggie's hand, sounding weary to the bone. 'I'm Maggie's husband. And this is Leonie, Maggie's sister, and her husband, Connor. This is Leonie and Connor's baby.'

'Maybe we need to get something straight,' Oliver said, gently but still firmly. He was focusing on Maggie, talking to the room in general but holding the exhausted woman's gaze with his. 'This baby may well be Leonie and Connor's when it's born, but right now it has to be Maggie's. Maggie needs to own this baby if she's going to give birth successfully. And I'm looking at Maggie's exhaustion level and I'm thinking we need to clear the room. She needs some space.'

'But it's our baby.' Leonie looked horrified. 'Maggie's agreed—'

'To bear a baby for you,' he finished for her. Em was watching him, warily now, waiting to see where he was going. 'But right now Maggie's body's saying it's hers and her body needs that belief if she's to have a strong labour. I'm sorry, Leonie and Connor, but unless you want your sister to have a Caesarean, I need you to leave.'

'We can't leave,' Leonie gasped. 'We need to see her born.'

'You may well—if it's okay with Maggie.' They were in one of the teaching suites, geared to help train students. It had a mirror to one side. 'Maggie, that's an observation window, with one-way glass. Is it okay if your sister and her husband move into there?'

'No.' Leonie frowned at Oliver but the look on both Maggie and Rob's faces was one of relief.

'I just…need…to go at my own pace,' Maggie whispered.

'But I want to be the first one to hold our baby,' Leonie snapped, and Oliver bit his tongue to stop himself snapping back. This situation was fraught. He could understand that sisterly love was being put on the back burner in the face of the enormity of their baby's birth, but his responsibility was for Maggie and her baby's health. Anything else had to come second.

'What Maggie is doing for you is one of the most generous gifts one woman can ever give another,' he said, forcing himself to stay gentle. 'She's bearing your baby, but for now every single hormone, every ounce of energy she has, needs to believe it's her baby. You need to get things into perspective. Maggie will bear this baby in her own time. Her body will dictate that, and there's nothing you or Connor can say or do to alter it. If Maggie wants to, she'll hold her when she's born. That's her right. Then and only then, when she's ready and not before, she'll make the decision to let her baby go. Emily, do you agree?'

'I agree,' she said.

Em had been silent, watching not him but

Maggie. She was a wonderful midwife, Oliver thought. There was no midwife he'd rather have on his team, and by the look on her face what he was suggesting was exactly what she wanted. The problem, though, was that the biological parents exuded authority. He wouldn't mind betting Leonie was older than Maggie and that both she and her husband held positions of corporate power. Here they looked like they'd been using their authority to push Maggie, and they wouldn't have listened to Em.

Isla had sent him in for a reason. If this had been a normal delivery then Em could have coped alone, but with the level of Maggie's exhaustion it was getting less likely to be a normal delivery.

Sometimes there were advantages to having the word *Doctor* in front of his name. Sometimes there were advantages to being a surgeon, to having given lectures to some of the most competent doctors in the world, to have the gravitas of professional clout behind him.

Sometimes it behoved a doctor to invoke his power, too.

'Maggie, would you like to have a break from too many people?' he asked now.

And Maggie looked up at him, her eyes brimming with gratitude. 'I... Yes. I mean, I always said that Leonie could be here but—'

'But your body needs peace,' Oliver said. He walked to the door and pulled it wide. 'Leonie, Connor, please take seats in the observation room. If it's okay with Maggie you can stay watching. However, the mirror is actually an electric screen. Emily's about to do a pelvic examination so we'll shut the screen for that so you can't see, but we'll turn it back on again as soon as Maggie says it's okay. Is that what you want, Maggie?'

'Y-yes.'

'But she promised...' Leonie gasped.

'Your sister promised you a baby,' Oliver told her, still gently but with steel in every word. 'To my mind, that gift needs something in return. If Maggie needs privacy in this last stage of her labour, then surely you can grant it to her.'

And Leonie's face crumpled. 'It's just... It's just... Maggie, I'm sorry...'

She'd just forgotten, Oliver thought, watching as Leonie swiped away tears. This was a decent woman who was totally focused on the fact that she was about to become a mother. She'd simply forgotten her sister. Like every other mother in the world, all she wanted was her baby.

She'd have to wait.

He held the door open. Leonie cast a wild, beseeching look at Maggie but Em moved fast, cutting off Maggie's view of her sister's distress. Maggie didn't need anyone else's emotion. She couldn't handle it—all her body needed to focus on was this baby.

'We'll call you in when Maggie's ready to receive you,' Oliver said cheerfully, as if this was something that happened every day. 'There's a coffee machine down the hall. Go make yourself comfortable while Maggie lets us help her bring your baby into the world.'

And he stood at the door, calm but undeniably authoritative. This was his world, his body language said, and he knew it. Not theirs.

They had no choice.

They left.

Em felt so grateful she could have thrown herself on his chest and wept.

The last couple of hours had been a nightmare, with every suggestion she made being overridden or simply talked over by Leonie, who knew everything. But Maggie had made a promise and Maggie hadn't been standing up to her. Em had had to respect that promise, but now Oliver had taken control and turned the situation around.

Now there were only four of them in the birthing suite. Oliver flicked the two switches at the window.

'I've turned off sight and sound for the moment,' he told Maggie. 'If you want, we'll turn on sight when you're ready, but I suggest we don't turn on sound. That way you can say whatever you want, yell whatever you want, and only we will hear you.'

'She wants to be here...' Maggie whispered, holding her husband's hand like she was drowning.

'She does, but right now this is all about you and your baby.' He put the emphasis on the *your*. 'Emily, you were about to do an examination. Maggie, would you like me to leave while she does?'

Em blinked. An obstetrician, offering to leave while the midwife did the pelvic exam? Talk about trust...

'But you're a doctor,' Maggie whispered.

'Yes,'

'Then stay. I sort of... I mean... I need...'

'You need Oliver's clout with your sister,' Em finished for her. 'You need a guy who can boss people round with the best of them. You've got the right doctor for that here. Oliver knows what he wants and he knows how to get it. Right now Oliver wants a safe delivery for your baby and there's no one more likely than Oliver to help you achieve it.'

He stayed. Maggie's labour had eased right off. She lay back exhausted and Em offered to give her a gentle massage.

He watched as Em's hands did magical things to Maggie's body, easing pain, easing stress.

Once upon a time she'd massaged him. He'd loved...

He loved...

Peace descended on the little room. At Maggie's request Oliver flicked the window switch again so Leonie and Connor could watch, but she agreed with Oliver about the sound.

As far as Leonie and Connor were concerned,

there was no audio link. Any noise Maggie made, anything they said, stayed in the room.

Maggie's relief was almost palpable, and as Em's gentle fingers worked their magic, as Maggie relaxed, the contractions started again. Good and strong. Stage two was on them almost before they knew it.

'She's coming,' Maggie gasped. 'Oh, I want to see.'

And Oliver supported her on one side and Rob supported her on the other, while Em gently encouraged.

'She's almost here. One more push… One more push, Maggie, and you'll have a daughter.'

And finally, finally, a tiny scrap of humanity slithered into the world. And Em did as she did with every delivery. She slid the baby up onto Maggie's tummy, so Maggie could touch, could feel, could savour the knowledge that she'd safely delivered a daughter.

The look on Maggie's face…

Oliver watched her hand touch her tiny baby, he watched her face crumple—and he made a fast decision. He deliberately glanced at the end of the bed and carefully frowned—as if he was seeing something that could be a problem—and then he flicked the window to black again.

He put his head out the door as he did.

'It's great,' he told Leonie and Connor, whose noses were hard against the glass, who turned as he opened the door as if to rush in, but his body blocked them. 'You can see we have a lovely, healthy baby girl, but there's been a small bleed. We need to do a bit of patching before you come in.'

'Can we take her? Can we hold her?'

'Maggie needs to hold her. The sensation of holding her, maybe letting her suckle, will help the delivery of the placenta; it'll keep things normal. Maggie's needs come first right now. I assume you agree?'

'I... Yes,' Leonie whispered. 'But we agreed she wouldn't feed her. I just so want to hold her.'

'I suspect you'll have all the time in the world to hold her,' Oliver told her. 'But the feeding is part of the birthing process and it's important. I'm sorry but, promises or not, right now my focus is on Maggie.'

Em's focus was also on Maggie. She watched while Maggie savoured the sight of her little daughter, while she watched, awed, as the little girl found her breast and suckled fiercely.

Her husband sat beside her, silent, his hand on her arm. He, too, was watching the baby.

Without words Em and Oliver had changed places—Oliver was coping with the delivery of the placenta, checking everything was intact, doing the medical stuff. This was a normal delivery—there was no need for him to be here—but still there was pressure from outside the room and he knew that once he left Leonie and Connor would be in here.

'You know,' he said mildly, to the room in general, 'there's never been a law that says a surrogate mother has to give away her baby. No matter how this baby was conceived, Maggie, you're still legally her birth mother. If you want to pull back now...'

But Maggie was smiling. She was cradling her little one with love and with awe, and tears were slipping down her face, but the smile stayed there.

'This little one's Leonie's,' she whispered. 'You've seen Leonie at her worst—she's been frantic about her baby and it was no wonder she was over the top at the end. But I can't tell you how grateful I am that you've given us space to say goodbye. To send her on with love.'

How could she do this? Oliver wondered, stunned. She'd gently changed sides now so the baby was sucking from the other breast. The bonding seemed complete; perfect.

'It's not like we're losing her,' Rob ventured, touching the little one's cheek. 'She'll be our niece and our goddaughter.'

'And probably a bit more than that,' Maggie said, still smiling. 'Our kids will have a cousin. My sister will have a baby. To be able to do this... She's not ours, you can see. She has Connor's hair. None of ours ever looked like this. But, oh, it's been good to have this time.' She looked up at them and smiled, her eyes misty with tears. 'Em, would you like to ask them to come in now?'

'You're sure?' Em asked, with all the gentleness in the world. 'Maggie, this is your decision. As Oliver says, it's not too late to change your mind.'

'My mind never changed,' Maggie said, serene now, seemingly at peace. 'While I was having her she felt all mine and that was how I wanted to feel. Thank you for realising that. But now...now it's time for my sister to meet her baby.'

* * *

'How could she do that?'

With medical necessities out of the way, Oliver and Em were able to back out of the room. Leonie was holding her daughter now, her face crumpled, tears tracking unchecked. Connor, too, seemed awed.

Rob was still holding Maggie but the two of them were watching Leonie and Connor with quiet satisfaction.

'Love,' Em said softly, as they headed to the sinks. 'I don't know how surrogacy can work without it.'

'Do you seriously think Leonie can make a good mother?'

'I do. I've seen her lots of times during Maggie's pregnancy—she's been with her all the way. Yeah, she's a corporate bigwig, but her life has been prescribed because she and Connor couldn't have children. Maggie seems the ultimate earth mother—and she is—but she and Leonie love each other to bits. I suspect the over-the-top reaction we saw from Leonie in there—and which you saved us from—was simply too much emotion. It felt like her baby was being born. She wanted what was best for her baby and everything else got ignored. Mums are like that,' she said simply. 'And thank God for it.'

'You really think she can look after the baby as well as Maggie could?'

'I have no idea. I do know, though, that this baby will be loved to bits, and that's all that counts.'

'She can love it as much as Maggie?'

'That's right, you don't think it's possible.' She lowered her voice to almost a whisper. 'It's a bleak belief, Ollie, caused by your own grief. Have you ever thought about counselling?'

'Counselling?' In the quiet corridor it was almost a shout. He stood back and looked at her as if she was out of her mind.

'Counselling,' she said, serenely. 'It's available here. We have the best people...'

'I don't need counselling.'

'I think you do. You have so much unresolved anger from your childhood.'

'I'm over it.'

'It destroyed our marriage,' she said simply. 'And you haven't moved on. I expected you to have a wife and a couple of your own kids by now. You were scared of adoption—are you worried about your reaction to any child?'

'This is nuts.'

'Yeah, it is,' she said amiably, tossing her stained robes into the waiting bins. 'And it's none of my business. It's just... I've got on with my life, Oliver. You kissed me on Saturday and I found myself wondering how many women you'd kissed since our split. And part of me thinks...not many? Why not?'

Silence.

She was watching him like a pert sparrow, he thought, as the rest of his brain headed off on tangents he didn't understand. She was interested. Clinically interested. She was a fine nurse, a midwife, a woman used to dealing with babies and new parents all the time. Maybe she had insights...

Maybe she didn't have any insights. Maybe she was just Em, his ex-wife.

Maybe that kiss had been a huge mistake.

Step away, he told himself. He didn't need her or anyone else's analysis. But...

'Em, I would like to see Gretta and Toby again.'

Where had that come from? His mouth? He hadn't meant to say it, surely he hadn't.

But...but...

On Saturday he'd sat on the beach and he'd held

Gretta, a little girl who had very little life left to her. He should have felt…what? Professional detachment? No, never that, for once an obstetrician felt removed from the joy of children he might as well hand in his ticket and become an accountant. Grief, then, for a life so short?

Not that, either.

He'd felt peace. He acknowledged it now. He'd sat in the waves and he'd felt Gretta's joy as the water had washed her feet. And he'd also felt Em's love.

Em made Gretta smile. He was under no illusions—with Gretta's myriad medical problems and her rejection by her birth mother, she'd faced spending her short life in institutions.

And watching Em now, as she looked at him in astonishment, he thought, what a gift she's given her children.

It was his cowardice that had made that possible. He'd walked away from Em, so Em had turned to fostering.

If he'd stayed with her maybe they could have adopted a newborn, a child with no medical baggage, a child Em could love with all her heart. Only he'd thought it wasn't possible, to love a child who wasn't his own. He'd walked away because such a love wasn't possible, and yet here was Em, loving with all her heart when Gretta's life would be so short…

Had he been mistaken? Suddenly, fiercely, he wanted that to be true. For he wanted to be part of this—part of Em's loving?

Part of her hotchpotch family.

'Oliver, there's no need—'

'I'd love to spend more time with Gretta.' He was wise enough to know that pushing things further at this stage would drive her away. The way he felt about Em…it was so complicated. So fraught. He'd hurt her so much… Make it about her children, he thought, and even that thought hurt.

Her children.

'What time do you finish tonight?' he asked.

'Six.'

'I'm still reasonably quiet and I started early.' He glanced at his watch. 'I should be finished by five. What say I head over there and give Adrianna a break for an hour?'

'Mum'd love that.' She hesitated. 'You could… stay for tea?'

'I won't do that.' And it was too much. He couldn't stop his finger coming up and tracing the fine lines of her cheek. She looked exhausted. She looked like she wasn't eating enough. He wanted to pick her up, take her somewhere great, Hawaii maybe, put her in a resort, make her eat, make her sleep...

Take her to his bed...

Right. In his dreams. She was looking at him now, confused, and there was no way he was pushing that confusion.

'I have a meeting back here at the hospital at seven,' he lied. 'So I'll be leaving as you get home.'

'You're sure you want to?'

'I want to. And if I can...for what time Gretta has left, if you'll allow me, it would be my privilege to share.'

'I don't—'

'This is nothing to do with you and me,' he said, urgently now. 'It's simply that I have time on my hands—and I've fallen for your daughter.'

CHAPTER ELEVEN

SHE SHOULD HAVE said no. The thought of Oliver being with the kids when she wasn't there was disconcerting, to say the least. She rang Adrianna and warned her and Adrianna's pleasure disconcerted her even more.

'I always said he was a lovely man. I was so sorry when you two split. It was just that awful time—it would have split up any couple.'

'We're incompatible, Mum,' she said, and she heard Adrianna smile down the phone.

'You had differences. Maybe those differences aren't as great as they once seemed.'

'Mum…'

'I'm just saying. But, okay, sweetheart, I won't interfere. I'll say nothing.'

Which didn't mean she was thinking nothing, Em decided as she headed to her next case. Luckily, it was a lovely, normal delivery, a little girl born to an Italian couple. Their fourth baby—and

their fourth daughter—was greeted like the miracle all babies were.

She left them professing huge gratitude, and Em
thought: How come the cases where all I do is
catch are the ones where I get the most thanks?
But it cheered her immeasurably and by the time
she went to see Ruby, her complications with Oliver seemed almost trifling.

Ruby was about to bring those complications
front and centre. The teenager was lying propped
up on pillows, surrounded by glossy magazines.
She had the television on, but she looked bored.
And fretful. She lightened up when Em came in,
and before Em could even ask her how she was,
she put in a question of her own.

'Emily, I've been thinking. You and Dr Evans
split because you couldn't have a baby. That's
what I guessed, but it's true, I know it is.'

Whoa! Hospital grapevine? Surely not. Sophia was the only one she'd told. Surely Sophia
wouldn't break a confidence and even if she had,
surely no member of staff would tell a patient
things that were personal.

'How—'

'I'm sure I heard it.' Ruby's eyes were alight

with interest, a detective tracking vital clues. 'When I was asleep. After Theatre. You and that other nurse were talking.'

Sophia. Em did a frantic rethink of what they'd talked about. Uh-oh.

'So I've been thinking. I've got a baby I don't want,' Ruby said, and suddenly the detective Ruby had given way to a scared kid. 'Maybe you could have mine.'

There was an offer. It took her breath away.

She plonked down on the bed and gazed at Ruby in stupefaction. 'Ruby,' she said at last. 'How can you think such a thing?'

'I can't keep it,' she said fretfully. 'Dr Evans says I have to stay in bed so I don't go into labour and it's driving me nuts, but it's giving me time to think. Ever since I got pregnant…first Jason said he didn't want anything to do with it, or me. Then Mum said she'd kick me out if I kept it. And I was pig stubborn—it just seemed so wrong. I thought I was in love with Jason, and when I realised I was pregnant I was happy. I wasn't even scared. I even thought I might make a good mum. It was only after that…the complications came in.'

'Most of those complications are over,' Em said

gently. 'Your daughter has every chance of being born healthy.'

'Yeah, but I've been couch-surfing since Mum found out,' she said fretfully. 'I had to leave school because I had nowhere to stay, and how can I couch-surf with a kid—no one's going to want me.'

'Then this isn't about adoption,' Em told her, forcing herself to sound upbeat and cheerful. 'This is all about plans for the future. We have a couple of excellent social workers. I'll get one of them to pop in and talk to you. She can help you sort things out.'

'But there are so many things…and if the baby's prem, which Dr Evans says is even probable, how can I cope with a baby? If she had a good home… if you and Dr Evans could look after her…'

'Ruby, leave this.' The girl's eyes had filled with tears and Em moved to hug her. 'Things will work out. You won't have to give away your baby, I promise.'

'But you need her. It could save your marriage.'

'My marriage was over a long time ago,' she said, still hugging. 'It doesn't need your daughter to try and mend it. Ruby, I want you to stop worrying about me and my love life. I want you to only think about yourself.'

Oliver arrived at Em's house right on five. Adrianna greeted him with unalloyed pleasure—and promptly declared her intention of taking a nap.

'When Em rang, that's what I decided I'd do,' she told him. 'The tea hour's the hell hour. If I can have a nap first it'll take the pressure off both of us when Em comes home.' She smiled and suddenly he found himself being hugged. 'It's great to have you back, Oliver,' she told him. 'And it's great that you arrived just when we need you most.'

He was left with the kids.

He carried them out into the soft autumn evening, stupidly grateful that Mike from next door was nowhere to be seen. Both kids seemed a bit subdued, pleased to see him, relaxed but tired.

The end of a long day? He touched Toby's forehead and worried that he might have a slight fever.

Katy next door had a cold. Had she or her kids spread it?

Maybe he was imagining things. He was like a worried parent, he thought, mocking himself.

He wasn't a parent. Not even close.

He had these kids for an hour.

He set them on the grass under the tree. Fuzzy the dog came out and loped herself over Gretta's legs. Gretta's oxygen cylinder sat beside her, a harsh reminder of reality, but for now there was no threat. A balmy evening. Warm, soft grass.

'Look up through the trees and tell me what you see,' he said, and both kids looked up obediently.

'Tree,' Gretta said.

'Tree,' Toby agreed, and he found himself smiling. Gretta and her parrot.

Together they were family, he thought. They were a fragile family at best, but for today, well, for today this was okay.

'I'm seeing a bear,' he said, and both kids looked at him in alarm.

'Up there,' he reassured them. 'See that big cloud? It has a nose on the side. See its mouth? It's smiling.'

Neither kid seemed capable of seeing what he was seeing but they looked at each other and seemed to decide mutually to humour him.

'Bear,' Gretta said.

'Bear,' Toby agreed.

'He must live up there in the clouds,' Oliver decreed. 'I think he might be the bear from "Goldilocks". Do you guys know that story?'

Toby was two, a tiny African toddler suffering the effects of early malnutrition as well as the scoliosis and scarring on his face from infection. Gretta was a damaged kid with Down's. 'Goldilocks' was way out of their sphere.

'Well,' Oliver said serenely, settling himself down. The kids edged nearer, sensing a story. 'Once upon a time there were three bears and they lived up in the clouds. Baby Bear had a lovely soft little cloud because he was the smallest. Mumma Bear had a middly sort of cloud, a bit squishy but with a nice high back because sometimes her back hurt, what with carrying Baby Bear all the time.'

'Back,' said Toby.

'Back,' Gretta agreed, obviously deeply satisfied with the way this story was progressing.

'But Papa Bear had the biggest cloud of all. It was a ginormous cloud. It had great big footprints all over it because Papa Bear wore great big boots and, no matter what Mumma Bear said, he never took them off before he climbed onto his cloud.

Mumma Bear should have said no porridge for Papa Bear but Mumma Bear is really kind...'

'My Emmy,' Gretta murmured, and he wondered how much this kid knew. How much did she understand?

My Emmy...

It had been a soft murmur, a statement that Gretta had her own Mumma Bear and all was right with that arrangement.

'Porridge,' Toby said, and Oliver had to force his thoughts away from Em, away from the little girl who was pressed into his side, and onto a story where porridge was made in the clouds.

And life was fantasy.

And the real world could be kept at bay.

Em arrived home soon after six, walked in and Adrianna was in the kitchen, starting dinner. She was singing.

Oliver's hire car was parked out the front.

'Where's Oliver?' she asked cautiously, and then gazed around. 'Where are the kids?' Had he taken them out? It was late. They'd be tired. Maybe they'd gone next door. But Katy had passed her cold on to her youngest. She didn't want them there, not with Gretta's breathing so fragile.

'Hey, don't look so worried.' Her mum was beaming and signalling out the window. 'Look.'

She looked.

The two kids were lying under the spreading oak in the backyard. Oliver was sandwiched between them. He had an arm round each of them and they were snuggled against him.

Fuzzy was draped over his stomach.

'You can hardly see him,' Adrianna said with satisfaction. 'It's an Oliver sandwich. He's been telling them stories. I went for a nap but I left my window open. He's an excellent storyteller. He makes them giggle.'

'They can't understand.'

'They can understand enough to know when to giggle. Cloud Bears. Porridge stealing. High drama. Lots of pouncing, with Fuzzy being the pouncee.'

'You're kidding.'

'He's adorable,' Adrianna said. 'He always was. He always is.'

'Mum…'

'I know.' Her mother held up her hands as if in

surrender. 'It's none of my business and I understand the grief that drove you apart.'

'It wasn't the grief. It was…'

'Irreconcilable differences,' Adrianna said
sagely. She looked out the window again. 'But
from this angle they don't look so irreconcilable
to me. You want to go tell him dinner is ready?'

'I… No.'

'Don't be a coward.'

'Mum, don't.' She swiped a stray curl from her
tired eyes and thought she should have had more
cut off. She needed to be practical. She wanted…

She didn't want.

'I don't want to fall in love with him again,' she
whispered. 'Mum…'

And her mother turned and hugged her.

'It's okay, baby,' she told her as she held her
close. 'There's no fear of that, because you've
never stopped loving him anyway.'

She came out to tell the kids dinner was ready.
She was looking tired and worried. She stood
back a bit and called, as if she was afraid of coming further.

Fuzzy raced across to her, barking. The kids

looked round and saw her and Toby started bee-tling across the lawn to her. The scoliosis meant he couldn't walk yet, but he could crawl, and crawl he did, a power crawl, his stiff legs making him look like a weird little bug. He was a bug who squealed with joy as Em swung him up in her arms.

Gretta couldn't crawl. She lay and smiled, waiting for Em to come and fetch her, and Oliver thought that, combined, these kids weighed heaps and Em was slight and...

And it was the life she'd chosen. The life she'd wanted as an alternative to staying married to him.

He rose, lifted Gretta and her oxygen cylinder and carried her across to Em. Gretta reached out her arms to be hugged. Oliver tried for a kid swap in midair and suddenly they were all squeezed together. Kids in the middle. Him on one side, Em on the other, Fuzzy bouncing around in the middle of all their feet.

It was a sandwich squeeze, he thought, a group hug, but he was holding Em. They were the wagons circling the kids. Keeping them safe?

Nothing could keep Gretta safe.

And then Toby coughed and Em tugged away with quick concern. 'Oh, no,' she whispered as she took in Toby's flushed face. 'Katy's bug...'

'I've had them lying on either side of me, and that's the first cough. In the fresh air it should be okay. Should we try and isolate them?'

'It'll be too late, if indeed it's Katy's cold. And besides...' Her voice fell away.

'Besides?'

'We made a decision, Mum and I. The first couple of years of Gretta's life were practically all spent in hospital. She was growing so institutionalised she was starting to not respond at all. Tristan's been her doctor from the beginning. After the last bout of surgery—it was a huge gamble but it didn't pay off—he told us to take her home and love her. And that's what we're doing. We'll be a family until the end.'

Her voice broke a little as she finished but her eyes were still resolute. 'She's Toby's sister,' she said. 'We know there are risks, but the fact that she's family overrides everything.'

'So you'll let her catch—'

'I'll do as much as I can to not let her catch whatever this is,' she said. 'Toby can sleep with

Mum and I'll sleep with Gretta so they're not sharing a room. We'll wash and we'll disinfect. But that's all we'll do.'

'That alone will take a power of work.'

'So what's the alternative?' she demanded, lifting her chin. 'Gretta's my daughter, Oliver. The decision is mine.'

Toby's cold was minor, a sniffle and a cough, no big deal. He was quieter than usual, but that was okay because it meant he was supremely happy to lie under the oak tree every evening and listen to Oliver's stories.

Because Oliver kept coming every evening.

'Why?' Em demanded on the third evening. 'Oliver, you don't need to. You owe me nothing.'

'This is little to do with you,' he said, and was surprised into acknowledging that he spoke the truth. For at first these kids had seemed like Em's kids, the kids he'd refused her, a part of Em. And at first he'd agreed to take care of them because of Em. It had been a way to get to know her again— and there was a hefty dose of guilt thrown in for good measure.

But now… He lay under the oak and the bears

became tortoises or heffalumps or antigowob-blers—that one took a bit of explaining—and he found he was taking as much pleasure as he was giving. And as much quiet satisfaction.

The last five years had been hectic, frantic, building up a career to the point where he knew he was one of the best in-utero surgeons in the world. It hadn't been easy. He'd had little time for anything else, and in truth he hadn't wanted time.

If he'd had free time he'd have thought about Em.

But now, with his career back in Australia yet to build up, he did have that time. And he wasn't thinking about Em—or not all the time, he conceded. He was thinking of two kids.

Of what story he could tell them tonight to make them laugh.

Of how to lessen the burden on Em's shoulders while acknowledging her right to love these two.

How had he ever thought she couldn't love an adopted child?

And as time went on, he thought...How could he have thought that of himself? These kids were somehow wrapping themselves around his heart like two tiny worms. They were two brave, damaged kids who, without Em's big heart, would be institutionalised and isolated.

These were kids who could well break her heart. Gretta's prognosis was grim. Once Toby's medical condition improved, the paperwork to keep him in the country would be mind-blowing.

It didn't seem to matter. Em just...loved. Her courage took his breath away.

Her love made him rethink his life.

What sort of dumb, cruel mistake have I made? he demanded of himself after his first week of childminding. What have I thrown away?

For he had thrown it. Em was always happy to see him, always grateful for the help he gave, always bubbly with the kids when he was around. But as soon as possible she withdrew. What would she say if he asked her to reconsider their relationship? He had no right to ask, he thought. And besides... How could he cope with the pain she was opening herself up to? To adopt these kids...

Except he didn't seem to have a choice. He might not be able to adopt them but, lying under the tree evening after evening, he knew he was beginning to love them.

As he'd always loved their mother?

* * *

Every night Em got home from work and he was there. Unbidden, Adrianna pushed mealtime back a little. So instead of coming home to chaos, sometimes Em had time to lie under the tree with them.

It became a routine—they greeted her with quiet pleasure, shifted a little to make room for her on the lushest part of the lawn, Fuzzy stretching so he managed to drape over everyone.

Oliver never tried to talk to her. There was no 'How was your day, dear?' He simply kept on with his stories, but he included her in them.

He found an Emily-shaped cloud and demanded the kids acknowledge it had the same shaped nose, and the same smile. And then he made up a story about Emily and the beanstalk.

It was better than any massage, Em conceded, lying back, looking up through the trees, listening to Oliver making her kids happy.

For he did make them happy. They adored this story time. Gretta probably understood little, but she knew this was story time. Lying on the grass, she was totally relaxed. Her breathing wasn't under pressure, she wriggled closer to Oliver and

Em felt her heart twist with the pleasure she was so obviously feeling.

And Toby... The scarring on his face had left the side of his mouth twisted. He had trouble forming words, but with Oliver's gentle stories he was trying more and more.

'And here comes the giant...' Oliver intoned, and Toby's scarred little face contorted with delight.

'S-stomp...stomp...stomp...' he managed.

And Em thought, How smart is my little son? And she watched Oliver give the toddler a high five and then they all said, 'Stomp, stomp, stomp,' and they all convulsed into giggles.

And Em thought...Em thought...

Maybe she'd better not think, she decided. Maybe it was dangerous to think.

What had her mum said? She'd never stopped loving him?

She had, she told herself fiercely. She'd thrown all her love into her children. She had none left over for Oliver.

But she lay and listened to giants stomping, she lay and listened to her children chuckling, and she knew that she was lying.

* * *

And she couldn't get away from him. The next morning she walked into Ruby's room and Oliver was there. Of course he was.

It seemed the man had slipped back into her world and was there to stay. He was an obstetrician, and a good one, so of course he was on the wards. He'd offered to help with Gretta and Toby, so of course he was at her house every night when she got home. He was the doctor in charge of making sure Ruby's baby stayed exactly where she was, so of course he was in Ruby's room.

It was just… Why did he take her breath away? Every time she saw him she lost her breath all over again.

She couldn't still love him, she told herself, more and more fiercely as time went on. Her marriage was five years past. She'd moved on. Oliver was now a colleague and a friend, so she should be able to treat him as such.

There was no reason for her heart to beat hard against her ribs every time she saw him.

There was no reason for her fingers to move automatically to her lips, remembering a kiss by the bay…

'Hey,' she managed now as she saw Ruby and Oliver together. She was hauling her professional cheer around her like a cloak. 'I hope Dr Evans is telling you how fantastic you've been,' she told Ruby. 'Because she has been fantastic, Dr Evans. She's been so still, she's healing beautifully and she's giving her baby every chance and more. I can't believe your courage, Ruby, love. I can't believe your strength.'

'She'll be okay,' Ruby said in quiet satisfaction, and her hand curved around her belly.

'We're going to let you go home,' Oliver told her. He'd been examining her, and now he was tucking her bedclothes around her again. 'As long as you keep behaving. Do you have somewhere to go?'

And Em blinked again. This was a surgeon—*a surgeon*—tucking in bedclothes and worrying about where his patient would go after hospital.

'Wendy, the social worker, has organised me a place at a hostel near here,' she told them. 'Mum won't let me home but Wendy's organised welfare payments. She's given me the name of a place that'll give me free furniture and stuff for the baby. It's all good.'

'You'll be alone.' Oliver was frowning. 'I'm not sure—'

'Wendy says the lady who runs the hostel has had other pregnant girls there. If I'm in trouble she'll bring me to the hospital. It sounds okay.' She hesitated. 'But there is something I wanted to talk to you about.'

She was speaking to Oliver. Em backed away a little. 'You want me to come back later?'

'No,' Ruby said, firmly now, looking from one to the other. 'I wanted you both here. I've been thinking and thinking and I've decided. I want you to adopt my baby.'

For Em, who'd heard this proposition before, it wasn't a complete shock. For Oliver, though… He looked like he'd been slapped in the face by a wet fish. How many times in his professional career had he been offered a baby? Em wondered. Possibly never.

Probably never.

'What are you talking about?' he asked at last. 'Ruby, I'm sorry, but your baby has nothing to do with us.'

'But she could have everything to do with you.'

Ruby pushed herself up on her pillows and looked at them with eagerness. More, with determination. 'I've been thinking and thinking, and the more I think about it the more I know I can't care for her. Not like she should be cared for. I didn't even finish school. All my friends are doing uni entrance exams this year and I can't even get my Year Twelve. I don't have anyone to care for my baby. I don't have any money. I'll be stuck on welfare and I can't see me getting off it for years and years. I can't give my baby...what she needs.'

'She needs you,' Em said gently. 'She needs her mum.'

'Yes, but she needs more. What if she wants to be a doctor—how could someone like me ever afford that sort of education? And there'll be operations for the spina bifida—Dr Zigler's already told me there'll be more operations. She'll need special things and now I don't even have enough to buy her nappies. And the choice is adoption but how will I know someone will love her as much as I do? But I know you will. I heard...when I was asleep... It was like it was a dream but I know it's true. You two need a baby to love. You split up because you couldn't have one. What if you have my baby? I could…I dunno…visit her… You'd let me do that, wouldn't you? Mum probably still won't let me go home but I could go back to school. I'd find a way. And I could make something of myself, have enough to buy her presents, maybe even be someone she can be proud of.'

'Ruby…' Doctors didn't sit on patients' beds. That was Medical Training 101, instilled in each and every trainee nurse and doctor. Oliver sat on Ruby's bed and he took her shoulders in his hands. 'Ruby, you don't want to give away your baby.'

Em could hardly hear him. Look up, she told herself fiercely. If you look up you can't cry.

What sort of stupid edict was that? Tears were slipping down her face regardless.

'I want my baby to be loved.' Ruby was crying, too, and her tears were fierce. 'And you two could love her. I know you could. And you love each other. Anyone can see that. And I know Em's got two already, but Sophia says you're round there every night, helping, and Em's mum helps, too, and she has a great big house…'

'Where did you hear all this?' Em managed.

'I asked,' she said simply. 'There are so many nurses in this hospital and they all know you,

Em. They all say you're a fantastic mum. And you should be married again. And it'd be awesome for my baby. I'd let you adopt her properly. She'd be yours.' She took another breath, and it seemed to hurt. She pulled back from Oliver and held her tummy again, then looked from Oliver to Em and back again.

'I'd even let you choose her name,' she managed. 'She'd be your daughter. I know you'd love her. You could be Mum and Dad to her. You could be married again. You could be a family.'

There was a long silence in the room. So many elephants… So much baggage.

Oliver was still sitting on the bed. He didn't move, but he put a hand out to Em. She took a step forward and sat beside him. Midwife and doctor on patient's bed… No matter. Rules were made to be broken.

Some rules. Not others. Other rules were made to protect patients. Ethics were inviolate. No matter what happened between Em and himself, the ethics here were clear-cut and absolute.

But somehow he needed to hold Em's hand

while he said it. Somehow it seemed important to say it as a couple.

'Ruby, we can't,' he said gently, and Em swiped a handful of tissues from the bedside table and handed them to Ruby, and then swiped a handful for herself.

The way Oliver was feeling he wouldn't mind a handful for himself, too.

Get a grip, he told himself fiercely, and imperceptibly his grip on Em's hand tightened.

Say it together. Think it together.

'Ruby, what you've just offered us,' he said gently but firmly—he had to be firm even if he was feeling like jelly inside—'it's the greatest compliment anyone has ever given me, and I'm sure that goes for Em, too. You'd trust us with your baby. It takes our breath away. It's the most awesome gift a woman could ever give.'

He thought back to the birth he'd attended less than a week ago, a sister, a surrogate mother. A gift.

And he thought suddenly of his own birth mother. He'd never tried to find her. He'd always felt anger that she'd handed him over to parents who didn't know what it was to love. But he looked at Ruby now and he knew that there was no black and white. Ruby was trying her best to hand her daughter to people she knew would love her, but they couldn't accept.

Would it be Ruby's fault if the adoptive parents turned out…not to love?

His world was twisting. So many assumptions were being turned on their heads.

He saw Em glance at him and he was pathetically grateful that she spoke. He was almost past it.

'Ruby, we're your treating midwife and obstetrician,' she said, gently, as well, but just as firmly. 'That puts us in a position of power. It's like a teacher dating a student—there's no way the student can divorce herself from the authority of the teacher. That authority might well be what attracted the student to the teacher in the first place.'

'I don't know what you mean.'

'I mean we're caring for you,' Em went on. 'And you're seeing that we're caring. It's influencing you, whether you know it or not. Ruby, we couldn't adopt your baby, even if we wanted to. It's just not right.'

'But you need a baby. You said…it'll heal your marriage.'

'I'm not sure what you heard,' Em told her. 'But no baby heals a marriage. We don't need a baby. Your offer is awesome, gorgeous, loving, but, Ruby, whatever decision you make, you need to take us out of it. We're your midwife and your obstetrician. We look after you while your baby's born and then you go back to the real world.'

'But I don't want to go back to the real world,' Ruby wailed. 'I'm scared. And I don't want to give my baby to someone I don't know.'

'Do you want to give your baby to anyone?' Oliver asked, recovering a little now. Em had put this back on a professional basis. Surely he could follow.

'No!' And it was a wail from the heart, a deep, gut-wrenching howl of loss.

And Em moved, gathering the girl into her arms, letting her sob and sob and sob.

He should leave, Oliver thought. He wasn't needed. He was this girl's obstetrician, nothing else.

But the offer had been made to him and to Em. Ruby had treated them as a couple.

Ruby had offered them her baby to bind them together, and even though the offer couldn't be accepted, he felt...bound.

So he sat while Ruby sobbed and Em held her—and somehow, some way, he felt more deeply in love with his wife than he'd ever felt.

His wife. Em...

They'd been apart for almost five years.

She still felt...like part of him.

Em was pulling back a bit now, mopping Ruby's eyes, smiling down at her, pushing her to respond.

'Hey,' she said softly. 'Hey... You want to hear an alternative plan?'

An alternative? What was this? Surely alternatives should be left to the social workers?

If Em was offering to foster on her own he'd have to step in. Ethics again, but they had to be considered, no matter how big Em's heart was.

But she wasn't offering to foster. She had something bigger...

'My mum and I have been talking about you,' she told Ruby, tilting her chin so she could mop some more. 'I know that's not the thing to do, to talk about a patient at home, but I did anyway. My mum lives with me, she helps care for my two kids and she's awesome. She also has a huge house.'

What...what?

'Not that we're offering to share,' Em said, diffidently now, as if she was treading on shifting sand. 'But we have a wee bungalow at the bottom of the garden. It's a studio, a bed/sitting room with its own bathroom. It has a little veranda that looks out over the garden. It's self-contained and it's neat.'

Ruby's tears had stopped. She looked at Em, caught, fascinated.

As was Oliver. He knew that bungalow. He and Em had stayed in it in the past when they'd visited Adrianna for some family celebration and hadn't wanted to drive home.

Josh had been conceived in that bungalow.

'Anyway, Mum and I have been talking,' Em repeated. 'And we're throwing you an option. It's just one option, mind, Ruby, so you can take it or leave it and we won't be the least offended. But if you wanted to take it...you could have it for a peppercorn rent, something you could well afford on your welfare payments. You'd have to put up with our kids whooping round the backyard and

I can't promise they'd give you privacy. But in return we could help you.

'The school down the road is one of the few in the state that has child care attached—mostly for staff but they take students' children at need. They have two young mums doing Year Twelve now, so if you wanted to, you could go back. Mum and I could help out, too. It would be hard, Ruby, because your daughter would be your responsibility. But you decided against all pressure not to have an abortion. You've faced everything that's been thrown at you with courage and with determination. Mum and I think you can make it, Ruby, so we'd like to help. It's an option. Think about it.'

What the...?

But they couldn't take it further.

Heinz Zigler arrived then, with an entourage of medical students, ostensibly to talk through the success of the operation with Ruby but in reality to do a spot of teaching to his trainees.

They left Ruby surrounded by young doctors, smiling again, actually lapping up the attention. Turning again into a seventeen-year-old?

They emerged into the corridor and Oliver took Em's arm.

'What the hell...'

The words had been running through his head, over and over, and finally he found space to say them out loud.

'Problem?' Em turned and faced him.

'You'd take them on?'

'Mum and I talked about it. It won't be "taking them on". Ruby's lovely. She'll be a great little mum, but she's a kid herself. She made the bravest decision when she chose not to terminate. It's becoming increasingly obvious that she loves this baby to bits and this way...we could maybe help her be a kid again. Occasionally. Go back to school. Have a bit of fun but have her baby, as well.'

'She offered it to you.' He hesitated. 'To us. I know that's not possible.' He was struggling with what he was feeling; what he was thinking. 'But if it was possible...would you want that?'

'To take Ruby's baby? No!'

'I was watching your face. It's not possible to accept her offer but if it was it'd be your own baby.

A baby you could love without complications. Is this offer to Ruby a second-best option?'

'Is that what you think?' She was leaning back against the wall, her hands behind her back, watching him. And what he saw suddenly in her gaze...*was it sympathy?*

'You still don't get it, do you?' she said, gently now. This was a busy hospital corridor. Isla and Sophia were at the nurses' station. They were glancing at Em and Oliver, and Oliver thought how much of what had just gone on would spin around the hospital. How much of what he said now?

He should leave. He should walk away now, but Em was tilting her chin, in the way he knew so well, her lecture mode, her 'Let's tell Oliver what we really think of him'. Uh-oh.

'You scale it, don't you?' Her voice was still soft but there was a note that spoke of years of experience, years of pain. 'You scale love.'

'I don't know what you mean.'

'You think you couldn't love a baby because it's not yours. That's your scale—all or nothing. Your scale reads ten or zero. But me...you've got it figured that my scale has a few more numbers.

You're thinking maybe ten for my own baby, but I can't have that. So then—and this is how I think your mind is working—you've conceded that I can love a little bit, so I've taken in Gretta and Toby.

'But according to your logic I can't love them at ten. Maybe it's a six for Toby because he'll live, but he's damaged and I might not be able to keep him anyway so maybe we'd better make it a five. And Gretta? Well, she's going to die so make that a four or a three, or maybe she'll die really soon so I'd better back off and even make it a two or a one.

'But Ruby's baby…now, if she could give her to me then she'd be a gorgeous newborn and I'd have her from the start and she'll only be a little bit imperfect so maybe she'd score an eight. Only of course, I can't adopt her at all, so you're thinking now why am I bothering to care when according to you she's right off the bottom of the caring scale? Baby I can't even foster—zero? So why are we offering her the bungalow? Is that what you don't understand?'

He stared at her, dumbfounded. 'This is nonsense. That's not what I meant.'

'But it's what you think.' She was angry now, and she'd forgotten or maybe she just didn't care that they were in a hospital corridor and half the world could hear. 'Yes, your adoptive parents were awful but it's them that should be tossed off the scale, Oliver, not every child who comes after that. I work on no scale. I love my kids to bits, really love them, and there's no way I could love them more even if I'd given birth to them. And I'll love Ruby's baby, and Mum and I will love Ruby, too, because she's a kid herself.

'And it won't kill us to do it—it'll make us live. The heart expands to fit all comers—it does, Oliver. You can love and you can love and you can love, and you know what? All that loving means is that you can love some more.'

'Em—'

'Let me finish.' She put up her hands as if to ward off his protests. 'I almost have. All I want to say is that you've put yourself in some harsh, protective cage and you're staying there because of this stupid, stupid scale. You can't have what you deem worthy of ten, so you'll stick to zero. And I'm sorry.'

She took a deep breath, closed her eyes, regrouped. When she opened them again she looked resolute. Only someone who knew her well—as well as he did—could see the pain.

'I loved you, Oliver,' she said, gently again. 'You were my ten, no, more than ten, you were my life. But that love doesn't mean there can't be others. There are tens all over the place if you open yourself to them. If you got out of your cage you'd see, but you won't and that has to be okay with me.' She pushed herself off the wall and turned to go. She had work to do and so did he.

'That's all I wanted to say,' she managed, and she headed off down the corridor, fast, throwing her last words back over her shoulder as she went.

'That's all,' she said again as she went. 'We agreed five years ago and nothing's changed. You keep inside your nice safe cage, and I'll just keep on loving without you.'

CHAPTER TWELVE

SHE SPENT THE rest of the day feeling shaken. Feeling ill. She should never have spoken like she had, especially in such a public place. She was aware of silences, of odd looks, and she knew the grapevine was going nuts behind her back.

Let it, she thought, but as the day wore on she started feeling bad for the guy she'd yelled at.

Oliver kept himself to himself. He was a loner. His one foray out of his loner state had been to marry her. Now he'd withdrawn again.

But now she'd put private information into the public domain. He might quit, she thought. He could move on. He hadn't expected her to be here when he'd taken the job. Would the emotional baggage be enough to make him leave?

She'd lose him again.

She'd told him it didn't matter. She'd told him she had plenty of love to make up for it.

She'd lied.

That was problem with tens, she thought as the long day continued. If you had a heap of tens it shouldn't matter if one dropped off.

It did matter. It mattered especially when the one she was losing was the man who still felt a part of her.

Her mother was right.

She still loved Oliver Evans.

He was kept busy for the rest of the day, but her words stayed with him. Of course they did. Tens and zeroes. It shouldn't make sense.

Only it did.

Luckily, he had no complex procedures or consultations during the day—or maybe unluckily, because his mind was free to mull over what Em had said. Every expectant mum he saw during the day's consultations…he'd look at them and think ten.

He wasn't so sure about a couple of the fathers, he decided. He saw ambivalence. He also saw nerves. Six, he thought, or seven. But in the afternoon he helped with a delivery. In the early stages the father looked terrified to be there, totally out of his comfort zone, swearing as he went in…

'This wasn't my idea, babe. I dunno why you want me here...'

But 'Babe' clung and clung and the father hung in there with her and when finally a tiny, crumpled little boy slipped seamlessly into the world the man's face changed.

What had looked like a three on Em's scale became a fourteen, just like that.

Because the baby really was his? Maybe, yes, Oliver thought, watching them, but now...with Emily's words ringing in his ears he conceded, not necessarily.

Afterwards he scrubbed and made his way back to the nursery. There was a premmie he'd helped deliver. He wanted to check...

He didn't make it.

A baby was lying under the lights used to treat jaundice. Two women were there, seated on either side. Maggie and Leonie. Surrogate mum and biological mum.

They didn't see him, and he paused at the door and let himself watch.

Leonie's hand was on her baby's cheek, stroking it with a tenderness that took his breath away.

Where was the tough, commanding woman of the birth scene? Gone.

Maggie had been expressing milk, the staff had told him. Leonie had paid to stay in with the baby, as his mum.

She looked a bit dishevelled. Sleep-deprived? He'd seen this look on the faces of so many new mums, a combination of awe, love and exhaustion.

Maggie, though, looked different. She'd gone home to her family, he knew, just popping back in to bring her expressed milk, and to see her sister—and her daughter?

Not her daughter. Her sister's daughter.

Because while Leonie was watching her baby, with every ounce of concentration focused on this scrap of an infant, Maggie was watching her. She was watching her sister, and the look on her face…

Here it was again, Oliver thought. Love off the Richter Scale.

Love.

Zero or ten? Em was right, it came in all shapes and sizes, in little bits, in humungous chunks, unasked for, involuntarily given, just there.

And he thought again of his adoptive parents,

of the tiny amount of affection they'd grudgingly given. He thought of Em and her Gretta and her Toby. He thought of Adrianna, quietly behind the scenes, loving and loving and loving.

He stood at the door and it was like a series of hammer blows, powering down at his brain. Stupid, stupid, stupid... He'd been judging the world by two people who were incapable of love outside their own rigid parameters.

He'd walked away from Em because he'd feared he'd be like them.

His thoughts were flying everywhere. Em was there, front and foremost, but suddenly he found himself thinking of the woman who'd given him up for adoption all those years ago. He'd never wanted to find her—he'd blamed her.

There were no black and whites. Maybe he could... Maybe Em could help...

'Can I help you?' It was Isla, bustling in, wheeling a humidicrib. 'If you have nothing to do I could use some help. I'm a man short and Patrick James needs a feed. Can you handle an orogastric tube?'

Patrick James was the baby he'd come to see. He'd been delivered by emergency Caesarean the day before when his mother had shown signs of pre-eclampsia. Dianne wasn't out of the woods yet, her young and scared husband was spending most of his time with her, and their baby son was left to the care of the nursery staff.

He was a thirty-four-weeker. He'd do okay.

It wasn't an obstetrician's job to feed a newborn. He had things to do.

None of them were urgent.

So somehow he found himself accepting. He settled by the humidicrib, he monitored the oro-gastric tube, he noted with satisfaction all the signs that said Patrick James would be feeding by himself any day now. For a thirty-four-weeker, he was amazing.

All babies were amazing.

Involuntarily, he found himself stroking the tiny, fuzz-covered cheek. Smiling. Thinking that given half a chance, he could love…

Love. Once upon a time he'd thought he'd had it with Emily. He'd walked away.

If he walked back now, that love would need to embrace so much more.

Black and white. Zero or ten. Em was right, there were no boundaries.

He watched Patrick James feed. He watched Leonie love her baby and he watched Maggie love her sister.

He thought about love, and its infinite variations, and every moment he did, he fell deeper and deeper in love with his wife.

She arrived home that night and Oliver's car was parked out the front. His proper car. His gorgeous Morgan. Gleaming, immaculate, all fixed. It made her smile to see it. And it made her feel even more like smiling that she'd yelled at Oliver this morning and here he was again. Gretta and Toby would miss his visits if they ended.

When they ended?

The thought made her smile fade. She walked into the kitchen. The smell of baking filled the house—fresh bread! Oliver's nightly visits were spurring Adrianna on to culinary quests. Her mum was loving him coming.

She was loving him coming.

'Mumma,' Toby crowed in satisfaction, and she scooped him out of his highchair and hugged him. Then, finally, she let herself look at Oliver.

He was sitting by the stove, holding Gretta in

his arms. Gretta wasn't smiling at her. She looked intent, a bit distressed.

Her breathing…

The world stood still for a moment. Still hugging Toby, she walked forward to see.

'It's probably nothing,' Adrianna faltered. 'It's probably—'

'It's probably Katy's cold,' Oliver finished for her. 'It's not urgent but I was waiting… Now you're here, maybe we should pop her back to the Victoria so Tristan can check.'

Congestive heart failure. Of course. She'd been expecting it—Tristan had warned her it would happen.

'You won't have her for very long,' he'd told Em, gently but firmly. 'Love her while you can.'

One cold… She should never…

'You can't protect her from everything,' Oliver murmured during that long night when Gretta's breathing grew more and more labored. 'You've given her a home, you've given her love. You know that. It was your decision and it was the right one. If she'd stayed in a protective isolette then maybe she'd survive longer, but not lived.'

'Oh, but—'

'I know,' he said gently, as Gretta's breathing faltered, faltered again and then resumed, even weaker. 'You love, and love doesn't let go.' And then he said...

'Em, I'm so sorry I let you go,' he said softly into the ominous stillness of the night. 'I was dumb beyond belief. Em, if you'll have me back...'

'Ollie...'

'No, now's not the time to say it,' he said grimly. 'But I love you, Em, and for what it's worth, I love Gretta, too. Thank you for letting me be here now. Thank you for letting me love.'

She was past exhaustion. She held and she held, but her body was betraying her.

Gretta was in her arms, seemingly asleep, but imperceptibly slipping closer to that invisible, appalling edge.

'You need to sleep yourself,' Oliver said at last. 'Em, curl up on the bed with her. I promise I'll watch her and love her, and I'll wake you the moment she wakes, the moment she's conscious.'

They both knew such a moment might not happen. The end was so near...

But, then, define *near*. Who could predict how long these last precious hours would take? Death had its own way of deciding where and when, and sometimes, Oliver thought, death was decided because of absence rather than presence.

Even at the time of death, loved ones were to be protected. How many times had a child slipped away as a parent had turned from a bed—as if solitude gave permission for release? Who knew? Who understood? All he knew was that Em was past deciding.

'I'll take your chair,' he told her, laying his hand on her shoulder, holding. 'Snuggle onto the bed.'

'How can I sleep?'

'How can you not?' He kissed her softly on her hair and held her, letting his body touch hers, willing his strength into her. This woman... She gave and she gave and she gave...

How could he possibly have thought her love could be conditional? How could he possibly have thought adoption for Em could be anything but the real thing?

And how could he ever have walked away from this woman, his Em, who was capable of so much love and who'd loved him?

Who still loved him, and who'd shown him that he, too, was capable of such love.

'I'll wake you if there's any change. I promise.'

'You do...love her?'

'Ten,' he said, and he smiled at her and then looked down at the little girl they were watching over. 'Maybe even more.'

She nodded, settled Gretta on the bed, then rose and stumbled a little. He rose, too, and caught her. He could feel her warmth, her strength, the beating of her heart against his. The love he felt for this woman was threatening to overwhelm him, and yet for this moment another love was stronger.

Together they looked down at this tiny child, slipping away, each breath one breath closer...

Em choked back an involuntary sob, just the one, and then she had herself under control again. There would be no deathbed wailing, not with this woman. But, oh, it didn't mean she didn't care.

'Slip in beside her,' he said, and numbly she allowed him to tug off her windcheater, help her off with her jeans.

She slid down beside Gretta in her knickers and bra, then carefully, with all the tenderness in the world, she held Gretta, so the little girl's body was spooned against hers.

Gretta stirred, ever so slightly, her small frame seeming to relax into that of her mother's.

Her mother. Em.

Somewhere out there was a birth mother, the woman who'd given Gretta up because it had all been too hard. Down's syndrome and an inoperable heart condition that would kill her had seemed insurmountable. But Em hadn't seen any of that when she'd decided to foster her, Oliver thought. She'd only seen Gretta.

She'd only loved Gretta.

'Sleep,' he ordered as he pulled up the covers, and she gave him a wondering look in the shadows of the pale nightlight.

'You'll watch?'

'I swear.'

She smiled, a faint, tremulous smile, and closed her eyes.

She was asleep in moments.

The quiet of the night was almost absolute. The only sound was the faint in-drawing of breath through the oxygen tube. Gretta's tiny body was almost insignificant on the pillows. Em's arms were holding her, mother and child ensconced in their private world of love.

Mother and child... That's what these two were, Oliver thought as he kept his long night-time vigil. Mother and child.

In the next room, Adrianna had Toby in bed with her. Whether Toby needed comfort—who knew what the little boy sensed?—or Adrianna herself needed comfort and was taking it as parents and grandparents had taken and given comfort since the beginning of time—who knew?

Adrianna's love for Toby was almost as strong as Em's.

Grandmother, mother, child.

He wanted to be in that equation, and sitting there in the stillness of the night, he knew he wanted it more than anything else in the world. What a gift he'd had. What a gift he'd thrown away.

But Em had let him into her life again. She'd allowed him to love...

Gretta shifted, a tiny movement that he might not have noticed if all his senses weren't tuned to her breathing, to her chest rising and falling. There was a fraction of a grimace across her face?

Pain? He touched her face, and she moved again, just slightly, responding to his touch as he'd seen newborns do.

On impulse he slid his hands under her body and gathered her to him. Em stirred, as well, but momentarily. Her need for sleep was absolute.

'I'm cuddling her for a bit,' he whispered to Em. 'Do you mind?'

She gave a half-asleep nod, the vestige of a smile and slept again.

He gathered Gretta against his chest and held. Just held.

The night enfolded them. This was a time of peace. A time of blessing?

Gretta was snuggled in his arms, against his heart, and she fitted there. Em slept on beside them.

His family.

Gretta's breathing was growing more shallow. There was no longer any trace of movement. No pain. Her face was peaceful, her body totally re-laxed against his.

He loved her.

He'd known this little girl for only weeks, and her courage, her strength, her own little self had wrapped her around his heart with chains of iron. She was slipping away and his chest felt as if it was being crushed.

Her breathing faltered. Dear God…

'Em?'

She was instantly awake, pushing her tumbled curls from her hair, swinging her legs over the side of the bed, her fingers touching her daughter's face almost instantly.

She just touched.

The breathing grew shallower still.

'Would you like to hold her?' How hard was it to say that? How hard, to hand her over to the woman who loved her?

But he loved her, too.

'I'm here,' Em whispered. 'Keep holding her. She loves you, Oliver. You've lit up our lives in these last weeks.'

'Do you want to call Adrianna?'

'She says she couldn't bear it. If it's okay with you…just us.'

Her fingers stayed on her daughter's face as Gretta's breathing faltered and faltered again. Gretta's frail body was insubstantial, almost transient, but Oliver thought there was nothing insubstantial about the power around them.

A man and a woman and their child.

'I wish I'd been here,' he said fiercely, though he still whispered. 'I wish I'd had the whole four years of her.'

'You're here now,' Em whispered as her daughter's breathing faltered yet again. 'That's all that matters.'

And then the breathing stopped.

They didn't move. It was like a tableau set in stone.

'Stop all the clocks...' Who had said that? Auden, Oliver thought, remembering the power of the poem, and somehow, some way it helped. That others had been here. That others had felt this grief.

Grief for parents, for lovers, for children. Grief for those who were loved.

Gretta had been loved, absolutely. That his own parents had doled out their love according to some weird formula of their own making—this much love for an adopted child; this much love for a child of their own making—it was nothing to do with now, or what he and Em decided to do in the future.

Their loving was so strong it would hold this little girl in their hearts for ever.

It would let them go on.

And Em was moving on. She was removing Gretta's oxygen cannula. She was adjusting Gretta's pink, beribboned pyjamas. She was wiping Gretta's face.

And finally she was gathering her daughter's body into her own arms, holding her, hugging her, loving her. And then, finally, finally the tears came.

'Go call Mum,' she managed, as Oliver stood, helpless in his grief as well as hers. 'She needs to be here now. And Toby... You need to bring him in, Oliver. For now, for this moment, we need to be together. Our family.'

They buried Gretta with a private service three days later. It was a tiny service. Only those who loved Gretta most were there to share.

Gretta's birth mother, contacted with difficulty, chose not to come. 'I don't want to get upset. You take care of her.'

'We will,' Em promised, and they did, the best they could. They stood by the tiny graveside, Oliver at one side of Em, Adrianna at the other, and they said goodbye to a part of themselves.

Such a little time, Oliver thought. How could you love someone so deeply after such a little time?

But he did. Years couldn't have made this love deeper.

He gathered Em into his arms afterwards and there were no words needed for the promises that were being made.

She knew and he knew. Here was where they belonged.

Katy had looked after Toby during the service— there were some things a two-year-old could never remember and couldn't hope to understand—but afterwards she brought him to them. 'Let's go to the Children's Garden,' Mike had suggested. 'The Botanic Gardens is a great place to play. That's where I think we all need to be.'

And it wasn't just Katy and Mike and the kids who arrived at the Gardens. Their hospital friends met them there, appearing unbidden, as if they sensed that now was the time they were needed. Isla and Alessi, Sophia, Charles, Tristan, even the obnoxious Noah—so many people who loved Em and knew the depths of Em's grief.

Heaven knew who was looking after midwifery and neonates at the Victoria, for at two o'clock on this beautiful autumn afternoon it seemed half the staff were here.

And suddenly, as if by magic, pink balloons were everywhere. They wafted upwards through the treetops and spread out. It seemed that each balloon contained a tiny packet of seeds—kangaroo paws, Gretta's favourite—with instructions for planting. Who knew who'd organised it, and who knew how many kangaroo paws would spring up over Melbourne because of Gretta? It didn't matter. All that mattered was that the love was spreading outwards, onwards. Gretta's life would go on.

There were blessings here, Oliver thought as he gazed around at the friends he'd made in such a short time, the friends that had been Em's supports while he'd been away, the friends who'd stand by them for ever.

For ever sounded okay to him.

* * *

Their friends drifted away, one by one, hugging and leaving, knowing that while friends were needed, alone was okay, as well. Sophia and Isla took Adrianna by an arm apiece. 'Rooftop Bar?' they queried, and Adrianna cast an apologetic glance at her daughter.

'If it's okay…I'd kill for a brandy.'

'If anyone deserves a brandy or three, it's you. I… We'll meet you there,' Em said, holding back, watching Oliver hugging Toby.

'Do you want me to take Toby?' her mum asked.

'I need Toby right now,' Oliver said, and Em blinked. Of all the admissions…

But no more was said. She stood silent until Sophia and Isla and Adrianna disappeared through the trees and they were alone. With her son. With…*their* son?

Then Oliver tugged her down so they were in their favourite place in the world, lying under a massive tree, staring up through the branches.

Toby, who'd submitted manfully to being hugged all afternoon, took off like a clockwork beetle, crawling round and round the tree, gathering leaves, giggling to himself. Death held no lasting impression for a two-year-old and Em was grateful for it.

'I think that's Gretta's nose,' Oliver said, pointing upwards at a cloud. 'I think she's up there, deciding whose porridge is hers.'

And to her amazement Em heard herself chuckle. She rolled over so her head lay on his chest, and his lovely fingers raked her hair.

'I love you, Em,' he said, softly into the stillness. 'I love you more than life itself. Will you let me be part of your family?'

She didn't speak. She couldn't.

She could feel his heart beneath her. His fingers were drifting through her hair, over and over. Toby crawled around them once and then again before she found her voice. Before she trusted herself to speak.

'You've always been my family, Oliver,' she said, slowly, hardly trusting herself to speak. 'Five years ago I was too shocked, too bereft, too gutted to see your needs. So many times since, I've rerun that time in my head, trying to see it as you saw it. I put a gun to your head, Ollie. Black or white. Adoption or nothing. It wasn't fair.'

'Even if your way was right? Even if your way *is* right?'

She could feel his heart but she could no longer feel hers. There'd been so many emotions this day... Her world was spinning...

No, she thought. Her world had settled on its right axis. It had found its true north.

'I'm so glad I came back in time to meet Gretta,' Oliver said softly, still stroking her hair. 'I'm so glad I was able to be a tiny part of her life. If I hadn't... She's a part of you, now, Em, and, believe it or not, she's a part of me. A part of us. Like Toby is. Like Adrianna. Like everyone is who released a pink balloon today. You're right, there is no scale. Loving is just loving. But most of all, Em, I love you. Will you take me on again, you and all your fantastic menagerie? Toby and Adrianna and Fuzzy and Mike and Katy and the kids, and Ruby and her baby when she's born? Will you let me love them with you? Will you let me love you?'

Enough. Tears had been sliding down her cheeks all day and it was time to stop. She swiped them away and tugged herself up so she was looking into his face. She gazed into his eyes and what she saw made her heart twist with love. She saw grief. She saw love.

She saw hope.

And hope was all they needed, she thought. Heaven knew how their family would end up. Heaven knew what crazy complications life would send them.

All she knew for now was that somehow, some way, this man had been miraculously restored to her.

Her husband. Her life.

'I can't stop you loving me,' she managed, swiping yet more tears away. 'And why would I want to? Oh, Oliver, I'd never want to. I love you with all my heart and that it's returned...well, Gretta's up there making miracles for us; I know she is.'

There was a crow of laughter from right beside them. They turned and Toby had a handful of leaves. He threw them at both their faces and then giggled with delight.

Oliver tugged Em to lie hard by his side, and then picked Toby up and swung him up so he was chortling down at them.

'You're a scamp,' he told him. 'We love you.'

And Toby beamed down at both of them. God was in his heaven, all was right in Toby's world.

He had his Em and now he had his Oliver. His Gretta would stay with him in the love they shared, in the love they carried forward.

Toby was with his family.

And two weeks later they went back to the gardens, for a ceremony they both decreed was important. For the things they had to say needed to be said before witnesses. Their friends who'd been with them in the tough times now deserved to see their joy, and they were all here. Even Ruby was here this time, carefully cosseted by Isla and Sophia but increasingly sure of herself, increasingly confident of what lay ahead.

Oliver had asked Charles Delamere to conduct this unconventional ceremony—Charles, the man who'd recruited him—Charles, the reason Oliver had finally come home.

Charles, the head of the Victoria Hospital. The man who seemed aloof, a powerful business tycoon but who'd released balloons for Gretta two weeks before. Who'd promised all his support, whatever they needed. Who'd also promised to move heaven and earth to cut bureaucratic red tape, so Toby could stay with them for ever.

But the successful bureaucratic wrangling was for later. This day was not official, it was just for love.

They chose a beautiful part of the garden, wild, free, a part they both loved. They stood under a tangled arch, surrounded by greenery. They held hands and faced Charles together, knowing this was right.

'Welcome,' Charles said, smiling, because what he was to do now was all about joy. 'Today Em and Oliver have asked me if I'll help them do something they need to do, and they wish to do it before all those who love them. Ten years ago, Emily and Oliver made their wedding vows. Circumstances, grief, life, drove them apart but when the time was right fate brought them together again. They've decided to renew their vows, and they've also decided that here, the gardens that are—and have been—loved by the whole family, are the place they'd like to do it. So if I could ask for your attention…'

He had it in spades. There was laughter and applause as their friends watched them stand before

Charles, like two young lovers with their lives ahead of them.

'Emily,' Charles said seriously. 'What would you like to say?'

They'd rehearsed this, but privately and separately. Oliver stood before Emily and he didn't know what she'd say but he didn't care. He loved her so much.

But then the words came, and they were perfect.

'Just that I love him,' Em said, mistily, lovingly. 'That I married Oliver ten years ago with all my heart and he has my heart still. What drove us apart five years ago was a grief that's still raw, but it's a part of us. It'll always be a part of us, but I don't want to face life's griefs and life's joys without him.'

She turned and faced Oliver full on. 'Oliver, I love you,' she told him, her voice clear and true. 'I love you, I love you, I love you, and I always will. For better and for worse. In sickness and in health. In joy and in sorrow, but mostly in joy. I take you, Oliver Evans, back to be my husband, and I promise to love you now and for evermore.'

He'd thought he had it together. He hadn't, quite.

When he tried to speak it came out as a croak and he had to stop and try again.

But when he did, he got it right.

'I love you, too, Em,' he told her, taking her hands in his, holding her gaze, caressing her with his eyes. 'Those missing years are gone. We can't get them back, but for now this is all about the future. We have Toby, our little son, and with the help of our friends we'll fight heaven and earth to keep him. As well as that, we have the memory of a baby we once lost, our Josh, and we have so many wonderful memories of our beloved Gretta. And we have all our friends, and especially we have Adrianna, to love us and support us.'

He turned and glanced at Adrianna, who was smiling and smiling, and he smiled back, with all the love in his heart. And then he turned back to his wife.

'But for now...' he said softly but surely. 'For now I'm holding your hands and I'm loving you. I love you, Emily Louise, as surely as night follows day. I love you deeply, strongly, surely, and I swear I'll never let you down again. From this day forth I'll be your husband. You hold my heart in the palm of your hand. For richer, for poorer, in sickness and in health, we're a family. But maybe...

not a complete family. I'm hoping there'll be more children. More friends, more dogs, more chaos. I'm hoping we can move forward with love and with hope. Emily Louise, will you marry me again?'

'Of course I will,' Em breathed, as Toby wriggled down from Adrianna's arms and beetled his way between legs to join them. Oliver scooped him up and held and they stood, mother, father and son, a family portrait as every camera in Melbourne seemed to be trained on them.

'Of course I will,' Em whispered again, and the cameras seemed to disappear, as their surroundings seemed to disappear. There was only this moment. There was only each other.

'Of course I will,' Em whispered for the third time, as they held each other and they knew these vows were true and would hold for all time. 'I'm marrying you again right now, my Oliver. I'm marrying you for ever.'

* * * * *

Don't miss the next story in the fabulous
MIDWIVES ON-CALL *series*
ALWAYS THE MIDWIFE
by Alison Roberts
Available in November 2015!